Letters of an Irish Publican

Letters of an Irish Publican

John B. Keane

THE MERCIER PRESS

The Mercier Press,
P.O Box, No 5, 5 French Church Street, Cork
24 Lower Abbey Street, Dublin 1

© John B. Keane

ISBN 0 85342 926 X
First published in 1974
Seventh edition 1992

Printed in Ireland by Colour Books Ltd.

To
Robert Howick
and to
Great Brewers
everywhere

Martin MacMeer the publican, mine host of Journey's End, a popular tavern in the village of Knockanee in the county of Kerry, initiates a series of letters to a friend in the city. Betimes he will epistolise to others. Harassed by the changing tempers and idiosyncrasies of his customers he bids to defeat frustration by noting their antics, mannerisms, virtues, faults and general behaviour. Underneath his counter, on a good-quality jotter supplied free by Guinness's Brewery, he would appear to be doodling the time away. In reality he is logging the arrival and departure of customers and faithfully recording their words and actions.

We should perhaps take a brief look into the background of Martin MacMeer. In most respects he is an ordinary publican committed to the serving of drinks hard and soft and committed too to the onerous task of having to listen to the problems, real and imagined, of all those who enter his premises. He is a bachelor by choice.

'I have no notion,' he was once heard to say, 'of becoming a martyr.'

A good figure of a man with a kind face he is now balding a little although women find him attractive. He is not easily ruffled but can be as short-tempered as the next when confronted with an awkward customer. When we find him in Journey's End he is past forty. He was not always a publican. In his eighteenth year he entered a seminary but on discovering that he was not cut out for the priesthood abandoned the idea altogether after two fruitless years and was fortunate to find a position with a newspaper.

Here he received some formal training as a reporter. As a result he was not long in acquiring the jaundiced eye of men who adhere to that occupation.

When Martin reached the manly age of twenty-five his widowed father tapped his last barrel and was called away to that place where all ales are clear and all spirits indisputably proof. Some weeks after his father's death he was summoned to town where the family solicitor promised to acquaint him with the contents of his father's will. Martin sat twiddling his thumbs in the waiting room wondering what lay in store for him. A maternal uncle who died prematurely some years previously had made a rather remarkable will which Martin remembered with some trepidation.

The name of the deceased uncle was Tom Long and the will was as follows : 'I Tom Long, being of sound mind, drank every penny I had before I died.'

There was no need for Martin to worry as he subsequently discovered. His father's entire possessions which consisted of a few thousand pounds and the inn known as Journey's End passed into his hands and so he became the proprietor of a public house. It is here we find him twenty years later putting pen to paper. He writes to a former colleague and friend from his newspaper days, one Daniel Stack, now a senior reporter with the same paper and as astute a judge of the human situation as one would be likely to find.

Journey's End,
Knockanee,
Co. Kerry.

Dear Dan,
The last time we met was in Ballybunion when we were both so drunk we should have been declared a danger to shipping. That was last summer two years ago. You suggested at the time that I should write a

book about an Irish publican. I doubt if I could ever come up with a book but from time to time I will forward, not for publication, a running commentary on the prevailing situation. Enough said for now. My love to Briege and the kids.

Your old sidekick,
Martin MacMeer.

Editorial Dept.,
The Irish Observer.

Dear Martin,
   Good to hear from you. Delighted you have decided to do a spot of writing. Why not change the names of the characters and the location and earn yourself a few pounds in the process. Whatever you decide I shall be looking forward to an inside look at public house life in rural Ireland.

In haste,
Dan.

Wellington Heights,
Dublin.

Dear Martin,
   I am the stout female solicitor who spent so many nights in your lovely pub during the summer. I am the one who used to play the piano and drink the green Chartreuse. I can do other things too but we will not go into those now. What I want is this :
   Could you find for me an old house, derelict or in reasonable repair which I might convert into a summer home near the sea at Knockanee. A place with a view would be ideal. If you can oblige I would appreciate if you would let me know and I will purchase provided the price is not too exorbitant.

I have fallen in love with Knockanee and the characters who live there all the year round. My eventual aim is retirement but that will be a long time yet. I must say I always found you most courteous, too bloody courteous as I recall when I called to say goodbye to you. Anyway do what you can for me.

Your sincere friend,
Grace Lantry.

Journey's End,
Knockanee,
Co. Kerry.

Dear Dan,
From where I sit I can see the rude Atlantic covered with white horses from point to point and off to its furthest horizons. On my right is Loop Head, drooping and lonely and on my left Kerry Head bull-necked and powerful. Between is a great plain of pure sea, churned and choppy now but in a few months time it will gently caress the browning, full-breasted bodies of young lovelies from distant cities. I must confess that I look forward to that time although I like this month of March the best of all. I like it for its promise and because it is neither summer nor winter. I love it for its freshness and if you want to know the sea for her true self March is the time to study her face and to fare where she holds court.

I see now that a brace of cormorants have entered the scene. They fly south in search of food, breasting the spitting seas of March. Gulls, of course, are mewing everywhere and there is a sting in the wind, a sting of salt, healing as a chest of medicaments and fresh as a kiss from a laughing girl. I know now that I could be happy nowhere else and I am glad I made that fateful decision to resign from the Observer.

Here comes the first customer of the day, a hard

case by name of Madge Dewley, the relict of a drunken schoolmaster and resident in a place known as Seaview Heights but known locally as Tipplers' Terrace. The inhabitants of this particular area would drink whiskey out of a pensioner's drawers with the difference that they will not be caught at it publicly. They are secret drinkers or so they think. Their neighbours could tell you to the drop what they have consumed.

Madge approaches the counter now bearing a brown message bag which contains three empty pint bottles. She smiles. I don't trust that smile. However, I will say this much for Madge Dewley. She is the soul of consistency. She never said a good word for anyone in her life, friend or foe, man or beast.

' 'Tis one right whore of a day, Martin,' she says.

' 'Tis all that,' I reply. She opens the message bag and withdraws the empty bottles which she places upright on the counter.

'Give us up three pints of stout,' she says. I do her bidding. While I draw the high stout and allow it to rest she explains her case as she always does. She knows I do not believe her but she lies as convincingly as ever.

'I'm making a couple of porter cakes,' she informs me for the thousandth time, 'one for myself and one for my sister Kate in Cork that married the postman.'

I keep drawing until the bottles are filled.

'How's Mrs Malone?' I ask for devilment, knowing they do not get on.

'The poor creature,' says Madge, 'she don't stop farting from one end of the day to the other. You'd swear you was next door to a machine-gun post.'

I cork the bottles and wrap them thickly with newspapers lest they break in transit. Madge produces another empty from her coat pocket.

'You can throw a half pint of whiskey in that,' says she, 'I'll be making a trifle tomorrow.'

I do as I am told and she pays me my dues.

'If you like,' I suggest, 'I'll send them up at lunch-time by one of the young Malones. They'll be passing from school.'

'No thank you,' Madge announces politely, 'breed, seed and generation of that crew drank drop down but they'll drink none of mine.'

Madge bids me the time of day and exits. I watch her small defiant figure as it braves the stormy weather. She pulls her hat tightly over her head and changes her booze bag from one hand to the other. Her supply will last for two days. She can't afford anymore. She is not poorly off. She has a modest pension and she lets most of her home to holiday-makers during the summer and autumn. I like her. I admire her. The only thing that will ever get the better of Madge Dewley is that which gets the better of every man and woman sooner or later. She pauses for a moment and rests the bag on the ground before ascending the stony path to Tippler's Terrace. Eva St. George, the landscape artist, in spite of the wind and the cold, descends with her trappings. Madge refuses to give way and Eva is forced on to the roadway. No saluta-tion passes between them. Eva will walk as far as the point and in the lee of the ruined castle com-mence a new painting. Nobody ever buys her paintings and her house from attic to basement is a jumble of canvases. Asked once for her opinion of Eva's work, Madge Dewley replied thus : 'I wouldn't allow her whitewash my lav, not if she was to pay me.'

Eva sees me through the window. She waves and I wave back. On her face is a look of radiance which says I will capture the tossing white waves to-day and the tumbling clouds and the glinting black rocks. If only she could paint. I'll close for the nonce. I'll be in touch. Love to Briege and the kids.

Martin.

12

Journey's End,
Knockanee,
Co. Kerry.

Dear Grace,
Re yours of Saturday last, I think I have discovered a place that might suit. It's perched high above the Point with a fine prospect of sea and coastline. It is dilapidated but not beyond repair. The owner is a man by name of Peadar Lyne. I suggested to him that he have it valued by an auctioneer and then to put a price on it. This way there would be no suggestion of chicanery and there can be no soul-searching later on. I think that it might be bought for three thousand. It stands on a quarter acre. A bit of gardening would do you no harm.

The reasons I was so courteous when you called to say goodbye last summer are as follows : It was three o'clock in the morning when you called and Father Pat Hauley the parish priest and his brother Father Ned, home from California, had you well-covered through the lounge window. I had them over for a few drinks since Father Ned was departing the following day for the States. Number two you were in bathing togs and that would be fine but for the fact that the upper piece was draped round your neck. Number three I never in all my born days saw anyone as drunk as you were then.

Hence the courteous reception. Try it again sometime and you may find me less hamstrung. I may be only a publican but I am not indifferent to the better things in life. It is too true that we, the publicans of Ireland, are the most lied about, the most abused, the most reviled of all God's creatures. Through the years we have been the sole target of fire and brimstone Resurrectionists and other itinerant, lusty-lunged missionaries belatedly loosed from their lonely cells and brimming with religious taspy. We have been

13

cursed by orphans and widows, damned by the wives and children of habitual drunkards and we have been consigned to eternal and exquisite agony by the mothers of this green and lovely land. Fair play to us it has all rolled off our backs like rainwater off a duck. The weaker amongst us have given in under the strain and the terrible injustice of it all. All is quiet now but let there be a disaster or an accident, a drowning or any damned calamity whatsoever and they'll pounce with a vengeance on the evergreen scapegoat i.e. your overworked Irish publican.

I don't know why I'm telling you all this. Why don't you drop down and see the cottage if you have a mind. There are no seas as capricious as the seas of March and no breezes as fresh or fair.

Yours sincerely,
Martin MacMeer.

Sandhill View,
The Old Mail Road,
Knockanee.

Dear Mr MacMeer,

I am aware that my husband John sometimes drinks in your pub. I am asking you in the name of God to serve him no more drink. He put us all out on the street the other night and when I tried to steal back into the house with the kids he struck me with his fist in the face and knocked me. This happens all the time when he has drink taken. Neither I nor my five children have ever enough to eat. The last time I bought shoes and clothes was at a jumble sale. I have stopped going to Mass. I am ashamed of my clothes and I am nearly always marked about the face. I can't leave him on account of the children. There is no misery greater than ours. Think of that, Mister MacMeer, the next time he asks for drink. I am also

writing to the five other publicans in Knockanee.
There is nothing personal.

Sincerely,
Mary Hauley.

Journey's End,
Knockanee,
Co. Kerry.

Dear Dan,
I have been blinded by a vision. I have been shattered from head to heel by the loveliest, sweetest
creature that ever trod the sands of Knockanee. She
was there under my eyes all the time but it took
divine intervention for me to behold her as she really
is, an angel pure and gracious, a fragile breath of
utter loveliness. Alas she is only eighteen and is spend-
ing her final year at the Convent here in Knockanee.
Her name is Antoinette Lingley. She is the daughter
of a local housing contractor. I swear to you, Daniel,
never was a fool of forty so woefully smitten. This is
my vision splendid. She is dark-haired, sloe-eyed and
willowy. Her skin is creamy and clear and she walks
like an olympic gymnast. She knows I exist because
whenever I salute her she smiles and winks. You'd
swear she knew my trouble. The mother, Lily, unfortunately, is one of the greatest straps ever to
dangle her legs over a golf club stool, a brazen, stuck-
up tit-tosser with a reputation for having popped in
and out of bed with any available buck more times
than she can actually remember. The father Jim
Lingley is a decent skin, a man you'd have to like.
He knows the score too but he loves Lily as he did the
day he said, 'I do.'
There is no figurine of brass as hard as Lily. She
has one abiding fear and that is your friend and mine
Madge Dewley. It is fear of Madge's tongue rather
than anything else. Lily was in the bar here one

15

morning last summer having a gin and tonic with Surgeon Casby from Cork. Casby wears white trousers, blue blazers, yellow socks and fawn suedes. He talks through his nose and finds it impossible to speak without first lifting his eyebrows to look down at a person. In short he is the epitome of snobbery and the kind that Lily has always desperately courted.

On the occasion Lily used her best Wimbledon accent and whenever old Casby squeezed her thigh she reacted by squeezing his. Half way through the second gin and tonic Madge walks in with her message bag. Making no attempt to conceal her business she addresses me in a loud voice.

'Martin, you son of a bitch, I'm in one hell of a hurry. Give me out three pints of porter. I am baking two porter cakes, one for myself and one for my sister that married the postman in Cork.' So saying she planks the three empty pint bottles on the counter. At the time Lily is telling Surgeon Casby about her childhood in the village of Kilseer. Suddenly Madge starts to sing raucously to herself. The surgeon and Lily look on nervously. Madge's song is about Kilseer. She addresses herself to Lily :

> Montana for cowpokes
> Newcastle for coal.
> Chicago for gangsters
> But Kilseer for your hole.

Poor Lily is mortified. Chuckling to herself Madge orders a half pint of whiskey for the mythical trifle. How such a mother as Lily could produce a daughter such as Antoinette is beyond me. I daresay natural goodness, like natural genius, will out at any cost. I will close for the present. I'll write again in a few days. Love to Briege and the kids.

As ever,
Martin.

Wellington Heights,
Dublin.

Dear Martin,
   You're a darling entirely. I'll try to pop down the week-end after next to have a look at Peadar Lyne's place. I enjoyed your letter but was somewhat disappointed when you closed with that dreadful piece of bull, yours sincerely. With bated breath I consumed your closing lines about the capricious seas of March etcetera. I was certain you were setting me up for a dirty week-end but then you went and spoiled it all with your yours sincerely.
   Anyway thanks for going to so much trouble. Do you think you could find me a place to stay overnight or are all the guesthouses closed for the off-season? I know the hotel is but you are well in the know and I'm sure you'll have no bother at all fixing me up.
                                        Yours sincerely,
                                        Grace Lantry.

P.S. I am a much soberer girl in the springtime.
                                        G.L.

Journey's End,
Knockanee.

Dear Mrs Hauley,
   I have just received your letter. You have no idea how upset its contents have made me. I will, of course, do as you request and refuse your husband drink when he calls again. I sincerely hope the other publicans will do the same. Indeed I am pretty certain they will. We are not a bad bunch even if we are painted otherwise. My dear Mrs Hauley, I would dearly love to help you. I could loan you some money. You need not worry about repayment for the present.

17

If there is anything in the world I can do please do not hesitate to call upon me.

Yours most sincerely,
Martin MacMeer.

Editorial Dept.,
The Irish Observer.

Dear Martin,

Is anything the matter? Just as I was beginning to enjoy those letters you suddenly stop. I was getting a tooth for your characters especially Madge Dewley. Your obsession with Antoinette Lingley is a natural phenomenon befitting your age. I have no doubt it will pass. Intransmutable as it may seem now there will come a time when you will smile at your present condition.

I hope nothing is amiss because seriously I am interested in finding out more about the good folk of Knockanee. Briege will be going to hospital shortly. Another natural phenomenon, the result of an error in judgement after the Journalists' Ball. I look forward to hearing from you within the week.

As ever,
Dan.

Sandhill View,
The Old Mail Road,
Knockanee.

Dear Mr MacMeer,

Please do not communicate further with me. If my husband knew I had written to you he would nearly kill me. He is too cunning to kill me outright. He would suffer for that. Please, for the sake of myself and my children, forget us.

Mary Hauley.

Journey's End,
Knockanee.

Dear Dan,
   Sorry for the delay between letters. The truth is
that I have had a fairly hectic time in the interim.
Easy for you to be dispassionate and philosophical
about Antoinette Lingley. You haven't even seen her.
She is the cause of many a backward look from
dotard downwards to juvenile delinquent. One of the
worst incidents to occur in the bar since I took over
happened last Friday night. I have been assaulted and
intimidated by gangs of youth on rampages and I have
survived onslaughts from the most vicious thugs during
the Whit and August week-ends but Friday night's
incident leaves these in the shade. Some time ago I
received a letter from a most unfortunate woman. She
asked simply to stop serving her husband with intoxicating drink. She had good reason to make such a
request, believe me.
   On Friday night at eight o'clock the bar was empty.
I sat looking out the window thinking futilely of
Antoinette and surveying the salty Atlantic all a
glimmer just then, swathed in gentle moonlight and
reflecting the glitter of a million stars. Ah my dear
Dan, there is no sea like the Atlantic. She is a thing
of a thousand moods. Turbulence, tranquillity, peace,
passion, savagery, serenity. They are all there. There
is no epic that would do her justice. She is too great,
too vast, too exotic. She is the empress of seas.
   While I sat there meditating I heard the door open
and then the deep voices of two males. Looking around
I saw that one was the husband of the woman who had
written to me, one John Hauley. He was accompanied by the chief thug of the district, a horrible
individual by the name of Joesheen Jameson. The
latter is a familiar figure in the country's leading jails.
His crimes chiefly consist of assault, theft and attempted rape to mention but a few.

Earlier in the week I had refused Hauley for drink but on that occasion he was alone and easy to handle. In fact he was as docile as could be and took my refusal quite well. Obviously it rankled him in the meanwhile because normally, bad as he is, he would not be seen in the company of a man like Jameson.

Instinctively I guessed that serious trouble was in the offing. I am without a phone and I never employ staff across the winter and springtime months. My regular customers, Peadar Lyne, Eva St. George and the others would not be arriving for an hour or so. I had no way of contacting the barracks and even if I had I wouldn't want to involve Mick Henderson the sergeant. He is due to retire next year. Alright if one of the two young guards was on duty but I happened to know that one was on holiday and the other strongly courting a girl in Tralee. No chance of catching him at home during his off duty period.

There was a lot of menace in Hauley's approach. He produced his pay packet and withdrew a pound. His opening reminded me of a poker player the strength of whose hand it is impossible to determine.

'I am calling,' said he in a deadly earnest fashion, 'for two halves of Scotch.' I looked at Joesheen who stood in the background. He wouldn't know Scotch from urine.

'Sorry,' I said, 'I cannot serve you.'

'I want to know why,' Hauley leaned across the counter and so did Joesheen Jameson.

'His money is as good as anyone else's,' Jameson put in.

'I want no arguments now boys,' I said calmly, 'and I want no trouble. If 'tis drink you really want there are several other pubs in the village where you'll get all you want.'

I figured if they left and were refused in the other pubs they might get into their heads that the whole village was against them. I could see, however, that they were already carrying a lot of drink, that I had been Judased by a fellow publican. It is the like of this particular Judas who gives us all a bad name.

'If you don't leave,' I lied, 'I'll send for the Civic Guards.'

Suddenly the pair unleashed a flood of expletives fouler than anything I had ever heard in my life. It was plain to see that Hauley's vanity had been severely pricked by my refusal earlier in the week. It must have festered. Word of such things spreads and trivial incidents assume new proportions. He works with Jim Lingley the contractor and naturally there was nasty banter on the site. I know what site chat can be like. Grown men can be exceedingly vicious.

Unexpectedly Hauley seized hold of a heavy ashtray and flung it at the shelf of bottles behind the counter. The ashtray smashed to pieces and two bottles of gin fell to the floor as a result of the impact. These also were smashed. Joesheen seized me by the tie and attempted to haul me out over the counter. I resisted easily. Hauley seized a small table and flung it at the shelves. Two more bottles, this time of whiskey, fell to the floor and were smashed. Hauley was berserk by now. The language still poured forth foul and filthy. He came across the counter. I decided it was time to evacuate. I vaulted across the counter and walked straight into a left hand swung wildly by Jameson. He caught me napping so much so that I almost fell. That settled it as far as I was concerned. He started to draw back his right hand to deliver the coup de grâce. My God he was cumbersome. I stepped inside him and smashed a good right into his mouth. I felt his teeth crunch. I stepped in closer as he reeled backwards and let him have a really good one in the same place. He sat on his arse without further ado.

Hauley, who was a witness to all this, had now lost all of his bravado. His face was pale. He knew I meant business. He ran round me with surprising speed and got through the door almost taking the damned thing with him. I contacted with my left shoe and felt it crack between the cheeks of his evil posterior. He ran down the street holding on to his gems, shouting in agony.

I lifted Jameson to his feet. It gave him all he could do to stand. I helped him outside and gave him a push in the general direction of his home. So much for that part of it. It is elementary for a fit man to handle half-drunks. Worse was to follow. I stood in the doorway and watched Jameson stagger his way homewards. He wouldn't forget his visit to Journey's End for many a day.

Meanwhile Hauley skulked in the shadows. I could see that he was still holding on to those which we all hold most dear. After a while, his condition improved, he entered the licensed premises of the widow McGuire's. I knew Kathy McGuire's form. She ran a good house. He didn't stay long. It was obvious that she had refused his request for drink.

The next place he tried was the Stella Maris guesthouse, a licensed premises next door to the widow's. He spent barely a minute there. It was gratifying to see that the other publicans of Knockanee were being faithful to Mary Hauley's instructions. This sort of treatment would soon send him home a chastened man and since he only acts up when intoxicated there was every reason to hope that his wife and children might have a respite from his tantrums.

His next port of call was the Hy-Brasil View owned by Dixie Megley. A minute passed and then two. Five more came and went, yet he did not re-appear. Dixie Medley then was the Judas. I locked up shop and went down the street. I entered Megley's and there I beheld John Hauley drinking a pint of beer. As soon as he saw me he skedaddled.

'What's the idea?' Dixie asked innocently from behind the counter.

'Don't you know?' I said.

'Know what?' he asked with the same innocence.

'Come off it, Dixie,' I advised him, 'you received a letter the same as the rest of us.'

'Look here, MacMeer,' he said coldly, 'I don't tell you how to run your business so don't tell me how to run mine. I have a family to rear and I serve who I like. If Hauley didn't get his drink here he'd get it elsewhere.'

'That's a lie,' I shouted. That was when I made my mistake.

'Don't raise your voice a second time in my premises,' he cautioned. 'If you do I'll send for the Guards.'

He had me there. There was much I wanted to say to him. I had a parting shot.

'If your livelihood makes you sink so low,' I said, 'you should abandon it.'

So saying I made my exit. I was depressed and down and out and I was in need of a stiff drink. I decided that I would not re-open my premises that night. As I was about to enter the widow McGuire's I was hailed by a soft, cultivated voice and at once I recognised the portly form of John O'Donnell, Guinness's representative for the area.

'My dear Martin,' said John, 'how good to see you out-of-doors. Shall we indulge in a quick one?'

I have always found John to be the most agreeable of companions. We entered the widow McGuire's together where we joined forces with the remains of a wedding party. A hearty sing-song followed and no more can I tell you if you were to give me the keys of the Kingdom of Heaven. My love to Briege and the kids. Her confinement can't be too far away now.

As ever,
Martin.

It should be revealed here that our friend Martin MacMeer is not above indulging in the occasional bout of sustained boozing. Four times a year and sometimes five he embarks upon what the good folk of Knockanee call a shaughrawn. Loosely translated and in drinking parlance this would mean a skite or batter. These shaughrawns usually end when the subject is physically exhausted and totally dehydrated by the ravages of continued drinking.

Martin MacMeer is no exception. After three or four days he may be seen sitting peaceably albeit drowsily in the lounge of a hotel in the town.

Having arrived at this near-comatose condition he waits silently for one of his friends to collect him. As a rule this act of mercy is undertaken by John O'Donnell of Guinness's or by Eva St. George or by Peadar Lyne. The last-mentioned it is who does it most often. Lyne is the owner of a pick-up truck. On the bottom of this he places an old mattress and thereon he dumps the exhausted body of his friend Martin. No word passes between them. In a day or so Journey's End is again open to the public and Martin MacMeer, mine host, would appear to be his old self.

Let me stress that he is no alcoholic. After such prolonged bouts of intense boozing he can return without difficulty to normal drinking habits, i.e. three and sometimes four pints of stout before retiring each night. The fact that he makes the occasional break is merely the Celtic extension of his character. This nomadic streak is a legacy from his Celtic forbears who once trudged across Europe and Asia in search of grazing and diversion.

The same legacy is inherited by all true Irishmen. But in some it is so dormant as to be everlastingly still. Slowly recovering he writes an imaginary letter to his beloved. He does not put pen to paper but speaks his heart to the listening sea.

Journey's End,
Knockanee.

My dearest Antoinette,
    You cannot know that for weeks past I have craved your company. It is I, Martin MacMeer, poet and publican, who calls out to you from the depths of his anguished and sorely-smitten heart. My love for you is a physical ache that hurts me day and night. In the darkness I see your young face shining like the Day Star. I imagine your dark hair falls and spreads and tumbles and tosses before my eyes.

    Oh how I wish it were winter when the hail drives noisily across the rooftops hammering at door and window and the bitter wind churns the seas to white foam. Oh to have you in my bed (wedded of course) under the starchy white sheets, to shelter you from the cold and the dark. Oh my lovely Antoinette, my spirit aches for your nearness. Gentle and pure as is my love the lust of my manhood cries out for your tender body. The well of my love is deeper than the deepest ocean. The strength of my love is stronger and fiercer than the wildest tempest. Oh how would I love you, my dream, my angel, my sweet rose petal.

    Do not think me an old fool of forty. There is more to me than that. There is the desire to cozen you through the nights and days of winter and spring and to help you bloom across the summer and autumn.

    What can I say to spell out my deep and lasting love for you? What new mixture of words can I spread before you, dear, enchanting schoolgirl? I see your moist red lips all day long. I feel your sweet breath upon my shoulder and oh those sloe-dark eyes that weaken my every resolve and enmesh me totally so that I am a witless captive fit for nothing but to grovel at your feet.

    Take pity on a fool of forty who through no fault of his own has been struck by the lightning bolt of

25

your heavenly beauty. Do not spurn me without thought. I am wounded enough as it is.

Your slave,
Martin MacMeer.

Editorial Dept.,
The Irish Observer.

Dear Martin,
   Your letters have become so erratic of late that I am concerned for you. I hope all is well. Is it the girl Antoinette? If it is please remember, my dear fellow, that she is but a transient fad of the forties. For God's sake keep in touch.

As ever,
Dan.

Editorial Dept.,
The Irish Observer.

Dear Martin,
   You might as well know now that I intend haunting you until such time as your letters complete the picture of life in Knockanee as seen through the eyes of a publican. Quite frankly I intend to use the letters as a base for a work of fiction so for God's sake get on with it. I can use the money. Briege came up trumps and produced a pair of twins, one of either sex. She sends her regards. Please write soon.

As ever,
Dan.

Journey's End,
Knockanee.

Dear Dan,
   Please forgive me for the delay in the letters. Use the bloody things for whatever purpose you like and

the best of luck to you. Under separate cover you will find a pair of suits for the new arrivals. I hope Briege thinks they're suitable. They were selected by a friend of mine, a lady from the big city, a solicitor by name of Grace Lantry who has been overwhelmed by the simple charms of this place and who is determined to settle down here.

To this end she has just planked down three thousand pounds for an old house, the property of my friend Peadar Lyne who no longer has any use for it since he came to live in the village itself. She spent last week-end here. I could not find suitable accommodation for her because it was off-season so she coolly announced that she would have no objection to staying here at Journey's End. I couldn't very well throw her out. Her visit, which I shall never forget to the day I die, coincided with Old Jimmy Cossboy's wake. Grace arrived at eight o'clock in the evening just as I was loading up Peadar Lyne's pick-up with the wake order, the biggest wake order I ever received incidentally. Since I was locking up to attend the wake I invited her along. She drank twice as much as anyone there and was a tremendous hit with the old lechers and the likes of those that were never within an ass's roar of a liberal-minded woman. I discovered that she had no religion of any kind. During the recital of the litany she chimed in with her own piece. There we were after the rosary, all kneeling on the floor, as sanctimonious a circle of arch-hypocrites as ever supplemented the obsequies of an unwanted old man.

'Holy Mary,' said the woman of the house.

'Pray for us,' we all answered dutifully. So it went on.

'Tower of Ivory,' said the supplicant.

'Pray for us,' we all answered.

'Bangers and mash,' said Grace Lantry.

'Pray for us,' answered the entire assembly. Need I say more about the effect she created? We arrived home drunk as sticks about half-past five in the morning. Peadar dumped us at the door. If you don't mind, she wanted to sleep with me. I pointed out that it was hardly the time and place and if you don't mind she says that she can't sleep alone. I asked her if this meant she was habitually promiscuous, and she neatly countered by explaining that she had a cat for company in her flat. I couldn't resist her. The woman is a veritable cannibal for sex. I won't be the better of her for a month. Nourishment I want at my time of life, not punishment. While I was tending bar she knocked around most of the time with Peadar Lyne but she failed to register there. Peader always claims that he was the only white man ever to screw a mermaid.

Says he, 'after jockin' a mermaid you'd never again have mind for ordinary women.'

When I reprimanded Grace for butting in during the Litany she told me that she thought it would only be right and proper to liven up the proceedings. Old Pettyfly, the well-known barrister, lives in retirement here for some years now. I introduced him to Grace and they had a great confab.

A few days later he waylaid me and I walking along the strand, trying to recover from the excesses of Grace and strong drink.

'That was a nice handful you introduced to me lately,' said he.

'Are all of your profession like that?' I asked jocosely.

'Not quite,' he said, but then he grew serious. 'I'll tell you one thing,' he confided.

'Yes,' I said eagerly.

'The law never stood back from it,' he said proudly.

You should have seen Grace at the Mass for Jimmy Cossboy. She did the opposite of what everybody else was doing. When all stood for the Gospel she sat down and when all sat down she stood up. It was plain to be seen that she was as foreign to the inside of a church as an unbroken colt to the starting gate.

She's gone back now but she will be calling regularly. She's too much for me. I'll have to think of something. I'll sign off now. Tomorrow is the annual Knockanee cattle fair. I'll be in touch.

As ever,
Martin.

Wellington Heights,
Dublin.

My Dear Martin,
I can't tell you how much I enjoyed last week-end. What a surprisingly shy and, of course, refreshingly chaste individual you are. I've never met anybody quite like you. Do all publicans know as much about human nature? I daresay they must being at the front line, so to speak, from morning till night.

I've been telling my friends about Peadar Lyne's exploits with the mermaid. Is there any truth in it? I think he was having me on. How does he manage when there are no mermaids? There is a divorcee who lives in the flat next to mine and she assures me that she would give the number one mermaid a run for her money any time.

There is so much more I want to say to you but it is very very wrong and very foolish to trust oneself to paper as many of my unfortunate clients know to their cost. I shan't do anything with the house this year but I expect to be coming into quite a sizeable sum next year from a paternal investment many years ago. I'll get down to business then. Meanwhile don't do anything I wouldn't do.

x x x x
Grace.

Journey's End,
Knockanee.

Dear Dan,
The Knockanee annual cattle fair has just ended
and presently permeating the entire scene, indoor and
out, is the smell of fresh dung. Before I describe the
day's happenings I want to put you a simple question.
When a lady appends a lot of kiss crosses to the end
of a letter is she being serious? Is there a special
significance? Is it commonplace?

Let me know as I am a man who values freedom
more than most. It was a great cattle fair with excellent prices. As usual they came in from the hinter-
lands with caps and ashplants and long coats, honest
men who would give you a lick of an ashplant as
soon as they'd look at you. True Celts every one.
There were only two fights in Journey's End and
these were mild enough compared with other years.
The other pubs had their fair share of rows but by
and large the violence would seem to be going from
cattle fairs. Most of the farmers, big and small, have
cars of their own now. They, and especially their
children, tend to be a little more sophisticated. Still
they retain many of their old features, some deplorably
bad, others upliftingly good.

I'll say one thing for your aged countryman in this
part of the world. He knows what frills are but he's
not a man for them. What a change they are from a
lot of the upstart new rich of today with their requests
for Scotch on the Rocks, Bloody Marys, Asses' Elbows
and what have you.

The first two customers to come in here this morning were middling-sized farmers from Cunnacanewer.

'Martin, my lovely boy,' said one of them, Mick
Hayes by name, 'throw us out two small ones.'

What a classically simple request, most endearing
to a publican's ears. Two small ones! They didn't ask
for Scotch or Irish or Canadian, just two small ones.

They couldn't care less as long as it was honest whiskey and if it wasn't honest they would not be long in telling you. It also shows that they trust the judgement of the publican to deliver a whiskey that should suit their particular tastes. In effect what they are saying is this : 'give us two halves of whiskey, Martin, a good honest whiskey that would suit the likes of us.' No illusions of grandeur here, no stupid pretensions. They are followed by others who call for the same. Each man will have four, maybe five halves of whiskey, no more. No force on earth will induce these men to have another whiskey. They regard the whiskey as a base for porter and a sound method of heating a cold interior.

After the whiskey it is your half pint of stout. They will drink that all day long, taking a short break now and then to inspect the cattle or to close a deal. They will make a long break in the middle of the day to visit Dolly Cotter's pieshop. There one can have a hot mutton pie immersed in rich, goodly soup. These mutton pies served thus are also regarded as a great base for porter. In addition to mutton pies they can have cold meat and tea or a plate of good boiling beef at Heffron's 'ating house. No embellishments needed here. An eating house is a place where you eat and should be so called.

The day wears on and deals are made. Subsequently countless libations are poured and there is a rough all round air of good fellowship. Of course the crowd is suitably interspersed with blackguards. These are loud and uncouth men who have disgusted their wives and children down the years. The only place they will be listened to is in a public house and believe me, Dan, it's no picnic for a publican to have to endure their curses and other crudities for the length of the day.

Sometimes I can't take anymore so I come from behind the counter and throw them out. They are never any use when faced with somebody their own size. I watch them too in mounting disgust when they try to insist on buying whiskey and brandy for men who don't want it. I never serve in cases like this. Fitter for these wretches to hand the money over to their wives. No fear. The dirty braggarts will drink, drink, drink till they can hold no more and then stumble home like 'cattle to abuse and manhandle their innocent families.

It is the Judases amongst us again who betray all humanity when they serve drink to sated monsters like these. Any decent publican will always stand up to these defilers of home and family.

Then there is the townland thug who tends to bully smaller men who have kept out of his way successfully until they meet at the pub counter. I have seen quiet, decent men humbled by these cowardly scoundrels.

I will not tolerate the presence of these men under my roof. I will serve drink to no man who will not show respect to me, to my house and to my customers. When a man comes into my pub he comes into a sanctuary and he is entitled to drink in peace.

I have seen bands of smelly young thugs from the bigger towns and cities trying to take over peaceful pubs in this little resort during the summer week-ends. They show no respect at all for age or sex. They want things their own way. Well they just can't have things their own way. They will behave and obey my rules or they won't be permitted to stay here.

A good pub is entitled to the same respect as a good home. I intend to see, no matter what the outcome, that it receives that respect.

As I say, Dan, the fair is over and there is now only the smell of droppings and the odd tuneless sing-song. Most of these farmers and labourers will go home happy, knowing a welcome from wife and children awaits them. Should anything happen them there would be tears and anguish in their wake. The grief would be indescribable.

What of the drunkard who abuses the sanctity of

his home? There would be no tears, nothing but a blessed, secret relief if he walked in his door no more.

I'm tired after the day. When I am occasionally very busy like this Madge Dewley gives me a hand in the kitchen, making sandwiches and the meals for myself and the part-time barman. She's getting old but she insists in coming.

I enjoy the cattle fair atmosphere. It is still a big event in the calendar of the Knockanee countryfolk. I fear, however, that it is passing from the scene and in your time and mine, Dan, the cattle will no longer be stood outside the doors of houses in the public street. Progress will put an end to it all, the way it put an end to an honest day's work and outdoor piddling.

I'll close for the present. Do not forget to answer the question concerning the kiss crosses. It may not seem important to you but to me it could be a matter of life and death.

Hold everything. She's after coming into my house. She approaches my humble counter with a heavenly smile on her radiant young face. Her eyebrows droop over her dark eyes. She blushes modestly. I swear that the blood has left my face and that time stands still. Oh God how I would love to hold that pale, lovely face in my hands.

'A bottle of gin please, Martin. It's for my mother. She'll fix with you herself. Oh and I nearly forgot. A half dozen bottles of tonic water.' You have guessed who it is. Antoinette of course. I fumble for the gin and the smaller bottles of tonic. I allow a bottle to fall from my hand. I nearly fall over myself trying to recover it. Oh what a hapless fool of forty am I. I find a box and wrap the bottles over and over with pages from old newspapers. I stall for time with futile questions about the weather. I ask her how her studies are going and other polite, needless queries. All the things I had planned to say are stuck in my throat. With a celestial smile she is gone. The place is like a shrine but barely vacated by a beatific vision.

Oh you pitiful fool who should and could have spoken your mind. What matter if she burst out laughing. The thing would be forever said and on second and third thoughts she would maybe come to reconsider you.

My claim would be staked and even if I never struck gold at least she would know how I felt about her. How many are there in the world who suffer the way I do?

I'll abandon this epistle for the moment. You'll hear from me soon.

As ever,
Martin.

Peadar Lyne writes to Grace Lantry in answer to a letter she has sent him. It is the first letter Peadar has ever received from a body revolving in such an outward sphere. It is confidential. In it she declares her love for Martin of Journey's End and requests Peadar to put in a good word for her whenever he can without, at the same time, letting Martin know her intent. She explains that a direct approach might frighten him away. She also questions him about the mermaid.

Sleepy Valley,
Knockanee,
Co. Kerry.

Dear Grace,

So you want to be his grace before and after meals and always with the greatest attention and devotion no full stops or commas or like hold-ups that get in my way dodge the fences and keep going to the post Ill hop a ball now and then but offers no hope hes dyed in the wool bachelor with notions of young wans like all that age last kick if you know what I mean still no harm keep trying ah the mermaid seen likely

droppings wan morning comin from seven Mass says
I mermaids for sure and after trailin awhile seen her
sittin combin her hair on a rock near Knockanee
Point just ablow the castle whistled her and she
turned she was on the point of divin toughen says I
the days long mounted no bother in the world the
finest ever straddled kept shakin her tail the whole
time wanted me go in the water and do it there good
job I was bate Id be in with her to my watery grave
like many a sailor She gets nasty when I wont jump in
flakes my oul man with a belt of the tail to this day
scales on it as my mother in the grave. I never seen
her after searched up and down from the Point to
Donnellys Rock but no trace. One flake of a mermaid
and no woman ever satisfies from the only white man
ever hammered a job on a mermaid.

                                        Peadar Lyne.

P.S. Try coaxiorum with Martin.

Editorial Dept.,
The Irish Observer.

Dear Martin,
    Many thanks for your long letter concerning the
Knockanee cattle fair. It is important to record events
like these if, as you say, they are in danger of disappearing from the scene. All goes well here. Briege
and the new arrivals are fine. She says the lady
solicitor has good taste. We both appreciate your
thoughtfulness in purchasing the gifts.
    You ask about the significance of kiss crosses. I
would not take them too seriously. For years I harm-
lessly corresponded with a number of girls and we
must have expended thousands of such crosses between us. On the other hand if she is not given to
lightweight statements you would want to watch your

step. One minute you are as free as the air and the next thing you know you're in hot water. It is a very tricky business any way you look at it. Women will use any and all lures in the matter of hooking the fish that suits their taste. All I would advise you at the moment is tread warily. Please keep writing me letters.

As ever,
Dan.

Demented from thinking of Antoinette Lingley the livelong day and indeed during most of his waking hours, Martin decides to confide his true feelings to his good friend Mother Martha, Headmistress of the Compassionate Convent School where Antoinette is a student. Over the years Martin has supplied the convent with bottled stout and brandy purely as tonics for the elders of the Compassionate community. The delivery of these items was always a most discreet mission and undertaken only by Martin himself. Even though the monthly order might be for a mere few glasses of brandy and a bare dozen of stout the number of eyebrows that might be raised by revelation of such deliveries would surely pass belief. Unfortunately, Mother Martha is in retreat when Martin calls. As a result he puts pen to paper.

Journey's End,
Knockanee.

My dear Friend,
I have no one to turn to but your good self who I trust and respect more than any woman I know. My plight is that I have fallen in love with one of your senior students, Antoinette Lingley. The feelings I store for her are pure in the extreme. Else I would not dare write to you. You can help me. Would it

be possible for me to speak to her in your presence? She is too young to be without a chaperone and we both know, alas, what her mother is like. Because of my age it is likely that her father may mistrust my motives. So it is to you I turn, dear friend. Can you see your way towards helping me?

Yours in J.C.,
Martin MacMeer.

Journey's End,
Knockanee.

Dear Grace,
Many thanks for your letter. I doubt if there is any truth to Peader Lyne's claim in connection with his mastery of the Knockanee Point Mermaid. On the other hand Eva St. George claims to have seen a mermaid one evening in June some years ago. The old people in Cunnacanewer maintain that June is the month when mermaids appear to humans. It was twilight when Eva saw her mermaid. The light was poor and she could easily have been mistaken. In the first place she is an artist and you must know, as a solicitor, the sort of hallucinatory testimony one can expect from such people.

In the second place early June is the time for the start of the peal salmon run. They move in their thousands from outside the estuary up to the spawning beds of the Feale and Shannon rivers. Needless to mention they are hotly pursued by hordes of hungry seals. I have no doubt that what Eva saw was a basking seal endeavouring to digest a suffocating feed of fresh salmon. If one is to believe in the existence of mermaids we might as well start believing in leprechauns as well.

Cynics around here argue that Peadar Lyne probably raped a seal on that memorable Sunday morning.

They say he was so drunk at the time that he could not tell the difference. It is well known that he was not returning from seven o'clock Mass as he claims but from a shebeen party in Cunnacanewer.

Some nasty-minded neighbour of his wrote an anonymous letter to Sergeant Mick Henderson demanding that Peadar be arrested and charged with self-confessed buggery.

So much for the mermaid. I am indeed glad you enjoyed your week-end. It was a nice break for you. Unfortunately, I will not be able to host you anymore. The summer season is now almost upon us and I'll want the rooms for the two girls I normally employ across the summer and autumn.

You'll have no problem, however, as most of the guesthouses will be open in five or six weeks' time and the hotel is due to unlock its doors on the first day of May. Then there is the caravan park if you had friends with you. You could always stay in the house you bought. It wouldn't be too bad in the summer if the place was properly aired.

You'll have no difficulty at all. I expect a very busy season so that I will have very little leisure time. In fact you could say that I will have no time at all.

Every good wish,
Your humble,
Martin.

Compassionate Convent,
Knockanee.

Dear Martin,
Where else would you turn in your time of trial and temptation but to your friends. I have read your letter carefully and burned it lest it fall into unsympathetic hands. We have a few pairs of those here, odd as it may seem. I am enclosing a prayer to Saint Jude. In future whenever you think of Antoinette I want you

to recite the prayer. In addition I want you to do the Stations of the Cross. Time and faith will heal your wound.

Yours in J.C.,
Mother Martha.

Wellington Heights,
Dublin.

Dear Martin,
  I fear I detect a certain note of coolness in your letter. There was no need to tell me about the re-opening of the hotel and guesthouses. I already know when they open. Remember I stayed in Knockanee last summer. You need not worry. I would not dream of imposing on you during your busy season. Have I said or done anything unwittingly to offend you? You must know I would not hurt you for the world.

  The tone of your letter worries me. Am I no longer welcome at Journey's End even as a customer? Please do not worry over me. I'm so depressed I could cry.

Love,
Grace.

Journey's End,
Knockanee.

Dear Mother Martha,
  Thanks for the Saint Jude prayer. I appreciate your advice about the Stations of the Cross too but I beg of you to intercede for me with Antoinette. You know my intent is honourable. All I ask is permission to speak to her in your own presence. What can be wrong with that? Will you please reply by return?

Yours in J.C.,
Martin.

Journey's End,
Knockanee.

Dear Dan,
I'm in a right kettle of fish. Grace Lantry has her
sights raised and is beginning to employ her womanly
wiles. I fear a stern struggle is going to be necessary
here and even at that, the outcome could be doubtful.
The other side of the picture is that I still crave
Antoinette Lingley. She means all the world to me.
What am I to do? Love to Briege and the kids.
As ever,
Martin.

Compassionate Convent,
Knockanee.

Dear Martin,
I do sympathise with you. I really do. I had better
begin at the beginning. If it were any other senior girl
I would intercede for you with her parents' approval
but in the case of Antoinette I cannot and will not.
Let me explain.
Our founder as you may know was Jean Marie
Colette McMangerton. On land willed to her by a
great-aunt she built our first humble retreat and with
the kind permission of the then bishop started her
community of fourteen sisters. That was in 1848 when
the need for an advanced form of education, not be-
littling the hedge schools, was sorely needed. The same
year saw the death of poor Dan O'Connell who won
Catholic emancipation for his people and was rewarded
ever after by the most vile and slanderous character
assassination. No Catholic would ever do the things of
which he stands accused.
To get on with it. For the past few years there has
been a steady decline in our numbers and so far this
year there has been no application for entry into our

novitiate. This may be purely a passing phase in our long and holy history but it could well be the death knell of the Compassionate Sisters.

There is still hope for us however. Antoinette Lingley is as angelic a child as ever drew breath and we have great hopes that she will join our order after she does her Leaving Certificate at the end of next term. She never wears minis or make-up but is as diligent a girl as ever sat in a classroom. She deserves a better mother than the one she's got. I have no wish to be uncharitable. The message I have for you is this, my dear Martin. Antoinette will not be the bride of any mortal man. She will be the bride of Christ as a Compassionate Sister. She has said nothing about it yet and maybe she does not know it yet but I know. I have the grace of God and I know she has it too. I am certain that any day now she will announce her decision to become one of us. It could be the turning point for the Compassionates. If a girl as pretty as Antoinette decides to become one of our company other girls may follow her example. I am sure she is an instrument of God.

I am so sorry, dear Martin. What about this girl from Dublin who stayed with you recently? We hear everything here, everything. God bless and keep you.

Yours in J.C.,
Mother Martha.

Journey's End,
Knockanee.

Dear Dan,

The reverend monther of the Compassionates in the local convent informs me that Antoinette is to become a nun. I cannot believe that a girl with eyes as mischievous as she will content herself shut away from the bright lights for the remainder of her life. I still long for her no matter what the reverend

41

mother says. I will wait and play my cards as they are dealt to me but holding my best trump for a final onslaught.

If you ever want to hear all the gossip and family scandals of a town or village keep away from the barracks of the Civic Guards. They have to search for news but whatever the reason people with spicy stories and family scandals make straight for the local convent. I would recommend the local convent to any investigator carrying out an examination of the town's inhabitants. The nuns know everything.

Here is the order in which I would place the best sources of information :

First . . . the convent.
second . . . the barber's.
third . . . the public houses.

The convents are omniscient. The barber's shop is fairly reliable and the pubs about fifty per cent accurate. There are other sources such as gossip shops and the various societies that constitute a town's activities, creameries or any place where people foregather in sufficient numbers. Believe it or not Mother Martha of the Compassionates knew that Grace Lantry stayed at Journey's End over the weekend I told you about. That's all she knows but like all women she has a bloody useful imagination with a finished intuition for drawing the worst possible conclusions. Yesterday I was delivering a bottle of brandy and a few dozen of stout. They give it to the old ones to help them sleep or to buck up the heart in the cold mornings.

'Were you at the Barbecue, Martin?' Martha asked.

'What barbecue?' I returned although I was responsible for supplying quite a large share of the booze and unfortunately, turned down an invitation to attend.

'Of course you weren't at it,' said Martha. 'I'd have heard if you were.'

Now I'm as curious as the next man and I must confess 1 had heard certain rumours. Eva St. George had mentioned it and Mick Henderson enquired if I had been at it. Madge Dewley in typical fashion announced that Sodom and Gomorrah were only trotting after it.

'I hear we have a nudist colony at last,' she said the other morning when she arrived for a half gallon of porter to make two porter cakes, one for herself and one for the sister that married the postman. That postman must have a right surfeit of porter cake by now.

According to Madge the most dreadful fornication took place. Eva St. George's account was less colourful. I knew that Mother Martha would have the true story. As it is the whole village and the entire county is literally buzzing with the news. Here is what actually happened. You have heard, no doubt, of Lochlune, the lovely wooded lake about three miles north of Knockanee. It's not really a lake, of course, and yet it's not quite a lagoon. It's composed of salt water and its levels depend on the tides.

Lochlune is a very beautiful place, more so at night when the moon shines on the waters and the winds rustle the leaves of the wild ash and laurel. It is a haven for courting couples who walk the lake shore in the long summer evenings. I often fancied myself walking hand in hand with Antoinette as the red sun sank slowly beneath the western horizon.

One thing is certain and that is Lochlune will never be the same again after the barbecue. Lily Lingley, the mother of Antoinette, imagines herself to be the C-in-C of the snob mob in this zone but it was Millie Dewey, the solicitor's wife, who thought up the idea of the barbecue. A few weeks ago she returned from a holiday with her sister Delia in Southern California. The place she chose was lovely Lochlune of my romantic fantasies. Millie Dewey threw the idea around and a committee was formed. Some of its members were Lily Lingley and Eva St. George who, because she is regarded as an artist, is always invited to whatever is happening. They decided upon the night of Saturday

43

last to hold the first ever barbecue in the district of Knockanee.

They had Dinny Pats, the local half-wit, out all day collecting driftwood for a great fire and generally preparing a site for the revels. The guests were carefully chosen, all the upper crust with the noble exception of that frigid few who are a bit too upper. I will deal no further with the preparatory details. The upshot of the whole business was that the entire affair was an utter disaster.

Knockanee was delighted as was all Cunnacanewer and the other townlands of this ancient barony. Most delighted of all were those who were not invited but who felt they should have been. At ten o'clock just as the party was sitting down to eat the rain came down in torrents. It came driving in from the west in great grey veils that made visibility extremely poor. The party was pretty drunk at this stage, all being nicely tanked up before attacking the grub. There was a wild scramble for shelter during which Lily Lingley was accidentally tripped. She fell headlong into Lochlune at its deepest point and narrowly missed being drowned. There was nobody sober enough to rescue her. She managed to clamber out. Dooney the dentist hit his head off a branch of a tree and had to receive eight stitches.

Millie Dewey, I feel sure, is sorry she didn't stay in Southern California. She had the hardest luck of all. She slipped on a slimy rock and fractured her hip after an unholy row with her husband. The car in which she was being driven to hospital skidded and crashed into a telephone pole. She broke her wrist and received two black eyes. I know and Mother Martha knows and all his friends know that Tom Dewey would never strike Millie but he is being blamed for both black eyes and no one believes the story about the crash despite the fact that the car is almost a write-off. People believe only what they want to believe. A group of seven people, including Dan Slatter the postmaster, rushed for the doubtful cover of a nearby sandhill when the storm broke. They could not have hit upon a less suitable place for lying on the sand in the lee of the dune was Dan's daughter Imelda and an obscure labouring boy who lived locally. They were not saying their prayers and they were not building sand castles. A bloody fight followed in which several became accidentally involved because of the dark and the teeming rain. Other groups joined in.

Fists flew and kicks were drawn. Nobody was sure what was happening. Most imagined they were being attacked by a group of outsiders. Consequently the safest course was to hit first and ask questions afterwards. Finally it wore itself out and the exhausted remnants of a once proud party straggled homewards.

They certainly gave the people round here something to talk about. The Lochlune barbecue will go down in history like the night of the big wind. All the casualties have not yet been counted and there are wild rumours of running duels between jealous husbands and over-zealous Casanovas. I'm certain there isn't a word of truth in this.

You may wonder how convents know so much. It is because sooner or later they are told everything. They are the repositories for the top secrets of the community. Over a drink one night in the lounge old Father Hauley, the parish priest, confided to me as follows : 'If I want to know something I go to the Compassionates. If they don't know I shorten my sails and end my quest for knowledge.'

On another occasion Mother Martha confided thus : 'They come to us for blooms and shrub branches for their altars and mantelpieces. We give freely. I suppose they feel they owe us something and endeavour to repay us with interesting titbits. It is an easy matter to sieve the grains of truth when one is an experienced assessor. We often hear as many as twelve versions of the same tale. Our experience helps us to deduce the true story from the whole collection.'

So you see, my dear Dan, the Spanish Inquisition never really ended. Still the Compassionates are harmless enough and their charges are as dear to them as life itself. The Lochlune Barbecue may have been a disaster for those involved but for the rest of us it was a heaven-sent diversion.

Lochlune deserves better of us mortals. You remember Callanan's romantic lake poem :

> 'Tis down by the lake where the wild tree fringes its sides
>
> The love of my heart, my fair one of heaven resides.
>
> I think as at eve she wanders its mazes along
>
> The birds go to sleep to the sweet, wild twist of her song.

Poor Callanan. He knew what love was too.

Peadar Lyne is right plank in the middle of one of his notorious week-long boozes. The curate here is a tiny, inoffensive man by the name of O'Dee. He takes a walk round the village at night and interferes with nobody. As I say he is diminutive in size and always walks warily.

Last night Peadar emerged from the Widow's at the same time that Father O'Dee was taking his midnight constitutional. Peadar was well and truly on the jigs after his third consecutive day on straight rum. His vision may have been badly blurred. Whatever it was he seized Father O'Dee by the throat and rammed him up against the Widow's front window. He was then heard to say : 'Give me your gold you rotten whore you.' Passers-by intervened but found it impossible to subdue Peadar who insisted he had captured a leprechaun. I now have a tough one to write to Grace Lantry so I'll close for the present. Love to all.

As ever,
Martin.

Journey's End,
Knockanee.

Dear Grace,
I assure you that you have offended me in no way.
I would be a churl indeed if I did not assure you of the
warmest of welcomes as always when you come for
your summer holidays. How you could think otherwise I cannot fathom. Be assured Grace of a seat at
my counter for as long as I am the proprietor of these
premises known as Journey's End.

The weather is greatly improved here. The local
news is of a barbecue that was held at Lochlune. Reports are exaggerated beyond words and there are
ungodly tales of rape, adultery and worse.

These reports are hotly denied by the participants
but nothing can now save them from the truly abominable tales that are in full circulation. Talk of this
barbecue has spread to nearby towns and God alone
knows how it will end.

I am sorry you were depressed when you wrote last.
That is life, isn't it, up one day, down the next. I know
what it's like. The things that get me down most are
funerals. No matter how awkward it is one is expected
to attend and it doesn't matter whether one was once
acquainted with the deceased or not. They take a lot
of my time and in the wintertime when they are most
abundant it means I have to close the bar to attend.
What difference does it make anyway? I'm sick at the
sight of gaping crowds round a hole in the ground.
Yesterday I made a vow. I shall forthwith cease to
attend funerals of all kinds. The next funeral to be
attended by me will be my own. All the publicans for
miles around are conspicuous at every funeral. I
suspect they attend for business purposes. I watch
them walking solemn-faced to the next of kin. Then
comes a long shake-hands and a longer, sadder shake
of the head to wring the full tragedy out of the occasion. I am sick of pretending to be sad, of shaking

hands with people I hardly know. Yesterday I attended my last funeral. I don't care who dies now. They'll be buried without me in attendance. Anyway there are so many publicans with nothing better to do that I shall hardly be missed.

From where I sit at this present time I can see Eva returning from her day's painting. She waves and I wave back. Here comes Peadar, red-eyed, wrinkled and shivering from stem to stern, like an ancient hooker that has lost every tack of its sail and ', at the mercy of mountainous waves.

'In the name of all that's good and holy,' he cries out, 'make me a hot whiskey as fast as you can.'

Madge Dewley arrives for a second cargo of booze. Today is pension day and she can indulge herself.

'Make it two hot ones,' Peadar instructs me with a badly broken voice.

'Stick it you know where,' says Madge, 'I want none of your drink.'

I will close now and see to their wants. Be assured that all is well between us. I regard you as a very dear friend and I would hate if anything were to damage that friendship.

Sincerely as ever,
Martin.

Wellington Heights,
Dublin.

Dear Martin,

I'm so glad all is well between us. You had me worried for a while. I thought it was all up. I am delighted to hear you say otherwise. It is so important to me that you have the same regard for me. Believe it or not I have already heard reports of the Knockanee barbecue. It's common knowledge here that a married man was stabbed to death but that it's being kept hush-hush. A colleague has also confided that two women

48

stripped naked after drinking too much and danced like dervishes round the barbecue fire. One is still in hospital after the beating her husband gave her. Has the body of the poor woman who was drowned been recovered yet?

Other people I've met over the past few days tell me of countless horrifying incidents straight from the lips of commercial travellers who have come direct from Knockanee.

One never knows does one? I would have thought that women of that age should have more sense. Yet I can understand what firelight and liquor might do to a middle-aged woman especially if she had been confined to her kitchen for a long period beforehand. Before I close, dear Martin, let me tell you once again what immense joy your letter has brought me. To put it mildly I would say that you have made my day. It is so worthwhile to have an understanding with someone like yourself. 'Bye for now.

xxxxxxxxxx
Grace.

Journey's End,
Knockanee.

Dear Dan,

It is as difficult to escape the clutches of Grace Lantry as it is for a salmon to shake off a hungry lamprey. I may have to plead the old religious issue if she gets any closer. That's one great advantage in being a Catholic when the opposing party is of another or no persuasion. Can you think of any other way I might shake her off? I would go as far as to plead insanity if needs be. As I said so often I treasure freedom above all else.

This is an astonishingly tenacious creature. She deliberately picks false meanings from simple straightforward statements. I am no match for her. That is why I call upon you to come to my aid. Think of something. Love to Briege and the kids.

As ever,
Martin.

P.S. : What do you say to telling her I am already married with a wife across the Irish sea in Camden Town or some other likely place?

M.

Editorial Dept.,
Irish Observer.

Dear Martin,

I have discussed your case with Briege and we are agreed that you should not lie to the girl. She deserves better, such as a simple thing called the truth. Just tell her you are determined to stay a bachelor, that you value her friendship but that a permanent legal union would not suit you. Once will do to tell her. Write soon.

Dan.

Compassionate Convent,
Knockanee.

Dear Martin,

I think it is but fair to tell you that Antoinette has left school and will not be coming back. Thereby hangs a long and harrowing tale but it is not for me to tell. It will be many a day before I get over the shock of what has happened. May God give me the strength to carry on. My faith has received a severe jolting. Maybe what happened was ordained by the almighty God to test me.

It will do you no good, Martin, to come looking for further information. I am entering a self-imposed retreat in an effort to recover my composure.

Too many parents have fallen down on the job and have left it up to us. We do what we can but we never can replace parents. Many of them are now content to look the other way. They have surrendered to rebellious offspring and go around pretending that all is well. They are the worst criminals of all, those parents who will not see.

There is now no cowardice worse than the cowardice of parents who will not face up to facts, who refuse to recognise that rearing children to be useful members of society is a full-time, complicated, sensitive vocation without parallel in the whole range of serious callings.

Failing a child is a transgression of truly great magnitude, so great that I know of no punishment to fit such a crime. I will close. It is just that I felt you ought to know.

Yours in J.C.,
Mother Martha.

Journey's End,
Knockanee.

Dear Dan,

Antoinette Lingley, the object of my love, is a fallen angel. She has been a fallen angel for some time. She was found out one day last week during the French class at the convent. Mother Martha teaches French and when she instructed the class to produce their Maupassant textbooks Antoinette Lingley who sits in the front seat right under Martha's nose was first to whip out her book. Alas and alack she also whipped out something else. It was in a package and what was inside was made of rubber.

'And pray what is this?' Martha asked as she recovered the package from the floor. She gently opened the package and produced the rubber object. Her face showed puzzlement. A girl in the back seat giggled but otherwise there was a ghastly silence.

'Well?' Mother Martha asked, growing somewhat annoyed.

'It's a balloon,' Antoinette Lingley announced.

'So it is,' said Mother Martha and she waved a mild finger of admonishment at her favourite. 'You are far too grown-up,' she chided, 'to be playing with balloons.' So saying she put the balloon in her pocket.

'Let us proceed with the first short story,' she said with a shake of the head and was rewarded with a beautiful smile from Antoinette. Some days passed and Mother Martha fell to thinking. Antoinette Lingley must have problems in the home if she resorted to balloons for playthings. Instinctively Martha blamed Lily Lingley. A great feeling of pity for Antoinette stirred inside her. She was determined to shelter the girl at all costs. A week passed and Doctor Sugan called to the convent to examine one of the older sisters. When the examination was complete he made his usual report to Mother Martha. Seizing her opportunity she mentioned Antoinette's interest in balloons. Sugan was on the point of dismissing the whole business as a girlish prank when suddenly a sly look crept over his face.

'What sort of balloon was it?' he asked.

'Just an ordinary balloon in a package,' Martha replied.

'You're sure it was in a package,' Sugan's worst suspicions were now almost confirmed.

'I have it right here,' Martha told him. She produced the package and handed it to the doctor. Sugan sighed as doctors are wont to do when confronted with the hard facts of life.

'' My dear Mother Martha,' said he sorrowfully, 'this is no balloon.'

'What is it then?' asked Martha.

'Pray be seated,' said Sugan.

That, my dear Dan, was how the *exposé* started. It is

now clear that Antoinette and the Lingley housemaid known locally as Kitty Bang-Bang entertained hundreds of young men from all over the country, from everywhere, in fact, except Knockanee. Antoinette ticked bottles of gin in every pub within a radius of ten miles and assured each publican that her mother would pay. Who would ever believe that a creature so beautiful would tell a lie?

My own balloon of innocent love is well and truly burst, Dan. Scandalwise it has almost equalled the Lochlune Barbecue.

Last evening Madge Dewley arrived for her cake and trifle ingredients. The customers present, including Peadar Lyne, were discussing the Lingley case.

'Kicky mare, kicky foal,' said Madge.

'Black cat, black kitten,' said Peadar.

No one said another word. I'll write soon. Love to Briege and the kids.

As ever,
Martin.

Wellington Heights,
Dublin.

Dear Martin,

I have to go abroad for a period on behalf of my company. I cannot say for sure when I will be back but I doubt if I will see Ireland this summer. There are a number of legacy problems to be sorted out and these will take time. What I am asking is this. Will you write to me when I am in the States? I will let you know where I will be staying. I doubt if I could endure the loneliness there if I did not hear from you regularly. I heard the story of the Lingley girl. I remember her. She used to lie near me on the beach at Knockanee. I always sized her up as a game piece, only awaiting her chance. Some of her posing would do credit to a professional. I can imagine her bamboozling a man with those dark eyes and that angelic smile. I'll be in touch as soon as I land in New York.

xxxxxxxxxx

Grace.

Journey's End,
Knockanee.

Dear Dan,

The summer season is only a few weeks away and already the ladders and the paint pots are everywhere. It's almost impossible to get a tradesman. The lovely Antoinette has left Knockanee and is, by all accounts, working as a receptionist with a doctor cousin of her mother's in Dublin. It is alleged that this doctor runs a very tight ship, rosary every night and Mass every morning not to mention pilgrimages to here, there and everywhere. Add to this a lights out stricture at ten-thirty and you will agree that Antoinette is in for different times. I still cannot get over it. Ah well. Life must go on.

As I write this I am also watching my uncle Matthew, my late mother's brother, as he engages in conversation with some of his neighbours from the hill country of Cunnacanewer. Matthew is a priceless old gent with a fabulous repertoire of yarns relating to his friends and neighbours. Did I ever tell you that this is a Cunnacanewer house? By this is meant that the folk of Cunnacanewer would not dream of drinking elsewhere when they visit Knockanee on business or for football matches or cattle fairs. The reason is, of course, that one of their women, my mother, was once established here as mistress of the house. In the case of the Widow McGuire's it is a house frequented chiefly by those from the northern end of Knockanee. The widow herself is one of the Dwans from the Point

54

so that no man from the Point or nearabouts will leave his business in other than the Widow's. Dixie Megley hails originally from Knockriddle and consequently his is a Knockriddle house.

Of the lot I would rate the Cunnacanewer crowd the cheeriest and the decentest. They can be shifty too and extremely clannish. At football games they have been known to attempt all sorts of wickedness including cheerfully endeavouring to kick a few referees to death as well as players on the opposing team and partisans. Not too long ago they castrated a chap from a nearby town. The reason was that the fellow raped a young Cunnacanewer girl working there. You will not be surprised to hear that, ever since, there is tremendous respect for Cunnacanewer girls wherever they go.

Otherwise the menfolk are a well-meaning lot with a great well of songs and folk tales. Nowadays it is common for women to patronise pubs but when I was a young fellow it was out of the question. Not so with Cunnacanewer women or indeed those from the other country townlands. They always drank with their men, mostly halves of hot port or whiskey. Their shawlies or poorer women who were not as well off as the farmers' wives would drink mulled porter the round of a Friday which is market day in Knockanee as well as being pension day. It is the busiest day of the week outside the high season time. They are well behaved in the pub and apart from spitting on the floor, spilling an occasional drink or puking without warning are model customers. Now and then they argue and on rare occasions they fight.

In their clannishness lies their strength. They love the pub. It is where they arrange to meet. If the women go shopping their parcels are delivered to Journey's End where they collect them later. They just would not think of entering another pub. I am one of their own so to speak and thus am worthy of their support.

Towards evening they will sing and maybe dance a few reels if an itinerant musician happens to chance by. This is the ultimate pleasure. Their type is fading fast. The shawls are disappearing one by one. The strong boots and the wellings are on the way out too as are the grey flannel, collarless shirts. My uncle Matt informed me this morning that an old woman who lives near him went on her knees to pray when she saw a Cunnacanewer turf-cutter going to the bog wearing low shoes and a collar and tie. There was a time, not so long ago, when such a garb of a weekday denoted only one thing. It meant that the wearer was on his way to court to answer a charge. The old woman rose from her knees when the man with the low shoes had passed and declared that the end of the world must surely be at hand when such flagrant profligacy was allowed to pass without punishment.

Grace Lantry is going to America. Thanks be to the Almighty God say I. She will be gone for the summer season and in a letter she told me that she would die with loneliness if I didn't write to her regularly. Talk about birdlime being sticky. How does a man release himself from the grasp of a determined woman? She misinterprets every line I write, always edging her way towards committing me to a marital direction. Love to Briege and the kids.

As ever,
Martin.

Journey's End,
Knockanee.

Dear Grace,
So you are off to America. Isn't it fine for you. I may not be able to write as often as I would like. In fact if the season is going to be as busy as I think I may not be able to write at all. When the day ends

I find myself fit for nothing but the bed. We will all be looking forward to seeing you when you come home.

As ever,
Martin.

Editorial Dept.,
The Irish Observer.

Dear Martin,
More please about your uncle Matthew and the colourful folk of Cunnacanewer. There must be thousands of tales to be taken down. A word of advice about Grace Lantry or indeed about any female who is unattached. If you must write a letter make certain you show it to a solicitor before you send it. I know far too many victims of thoughtless letter writing who would today be glad now to eat the paper on which they committed themselves for life. An ordinary man is no match for a scheming woman. Have the law on your side from this day forth whenever you put a pen to paper.

Briege is pregnant again after all our caution and care. We will definitely have to take positive steps after this. Don't forget to let me know more about Cunnacanewer. She sends her love.

As ever,
Dan.

Wellington Heights,
Dublin.

My dear Martin,
Thanks for your wonderful letter. I realise, of course, that you will not have time to write to me across the summer. Never mind. I'll write every day

to you. It is heartening to read that you look forward to seeing me again. I look forward to seeing you too and will head straight for Knockanee when I return.

When you go to bed exhausted during the summer make sure you go alone and think of me over in New York dreaming of you and the day when we shall be united again. I will be flying out early tomorrow morning and will write the moment I land. I must visit the pubs in New York and bring home all the latest techniques. I may be able to give you a hand behind the bar on occasion.

Do not worry about me while I am flying. I shall return safely and it will seem like no time at all.

xxxxxxxxxx
xxxxxxxxxx
Grace.

Journey's End,
Knockanee.

Dear Dan,

I have decided to ignore all future communications from Miss Grace Lantry. The next thing you know she'll have a halter slipped on me and I'll be another marriage martyr. Every word I have ever written to her she has miscontrued. She'll hear no more from me. Love to Briege and the kids. That's great news entirely about the new arrival or is it? About the people of Cunnacanewer. They were here again yesterday for the semi-final of the Kerry Junior League. The referee was knocked unconscious after deciding to abandon the game. Some onlookers were also hurt. By and large it was a quiet enough game when you consider that Cunnacanewer were matched against their arch-enemies Kilcogley.

Madge Dewley arrived after the game with her message bag. There was nothing but noise and confusion when she entered. When she approached the counter there was dead silence. She ordered four pints of stout for the porter cakes and a half pint of whiskey for the trifle. Not a word of any kind until she had left the premises. Astonishing you may think. Not so really. Madge already has had some runs-in with the Cunnacanewer crowd and they have a healthy respect for her as a result. I remember the last time the Cunnacanewer crowd were here she entered as usual and ordered the ingredients for the cake and trifle. As she was leaving a young chap spoke up.

'I hope you enjoy your bit of trifle, missus,' said he. Madge looked at him witheringly for what seemed like an hour. Then she spoke.

'That your rear exit might close up and fester,' said she. 'That it might break out under your arm and that you might have to take off your shirt to relieve yourself.'

Even by Cunnacanewer standards this was an outstanding curse. Hence the silence when she entered. The moment she left there was bedlam again. A row started between some Cunnacanewer boys and supporters of the visiting team. They entered Journey's End without thinking. In such cases I never interfere. It wouldn't do any good anyway. They wear themselves out in minutes and they are always contrite afterwards. They make it up with their foes and new friendships are established. That is the way with country people.

There is a backwoods retreat in Cunnacanewer called Cooleen. About a dozen or so families farm there and my uncle Matthew tells me that the married men emit loud, long shouts of exultation at the peak of their copulations. Since copulation usually takes place at night these shouts can often be heard all over Cunnacanewer.

A curate who once ministered there went around to the heads of the families in Cooleen and asked them to show some restraint as these audacious, nocturnal outbursts were the talk of the entire parish. He was told bluntly that their fathers and forefathers before them had shouted in triumph and exultation during such orgasms and they would continue in the old way until time came to an end or their seed failed.

An unusual development to the situation is best manifested in the following addendum by my uncle Matthew. Picture a peaceful night without trace of wind along the slopes of Cunnacanewer. The lights are out in every homestead and no man walks abroad.

Suddenly the peace is shattered by a mighty roar from the direction of Cooleen. Many are awakened instantly all over the hill and those who are not turn restlessly in their shaken slumbers.

At the base of the hill a man turns to his wife and speaks as follows: 'That's Mickeen Derry above in Cooleen. I'd know the voice anywhere. He's after a good cut tonight.'

This, according to my uncle Matthew, is commonplace and the minute a climax is heralded by a roar the identity of the man involved is known to all who are listening.

There was serious trouble once when the roar of a man living in a house in the south of Cooleen came instead from a house in the north of Cooleen.

'Ho-ho,' said all who heard, 'there's adultery rampant in Cooleen tonight.'

Truth to tell however there are only two recorded instances of misplaced roars in Cooleen over the last three generations. Potcheen was the cause of one and the other was an old buck of ninety who was only pretending. Only a fool would give himself away by roaring if he was misconducting himself.

Sometimes there are roars in the middle of the day but this is only where you have newly-weds. My uncle Matt maintains that as long as these roars are heard the future of Cooleen is assured.

I will close for the moment as I want to get a few early nights' sleep while I can. Love to Briege and the kids.

As ever,
Martin.

P.S. : Expect very little from me for the next few months, say until after the fifteenth of August, when things return to normal. The two girls who work with me for the summer arrive tomorrow. The season will begin in earnest then.

M.

Journey's End,
Knockanee.

Dear Grace,
Many thanks for your letter. Twenty-one pages takes a long time to read. That is why I am a month late in answering. The season here is at its peak. I am glad you are settled down nicely and falling into place. A retired American has come to live in Knockanee. He bought Christopher's great house beyond the Point. He must be aged eighty if he's a day. His name is Ernie Saschbuck. After making a pass at the Widow McGuire to which she did not respond he asked if there was a lunderin' house in the place. The widow told him she did not understand.

'You got a knockin' shop in this neck of the woods?' he asked. Still the widow did not understand.

'You know where I can find me a plain ornery cat-house?' Ernie tried another tack. Still the widow did not understand.

'Ma'am,' said Ernie, 'it sure does you credit you don't know what I'm talking about.' Since then he has settled in nicely. The parish priest Father Ned Hauley told me that he called to Ernie to remind him that his Station was coming up.

'What Station, man?' Ernie said. 'I'm here a month and I ain't even heard a train whistle.'

Still and for all when Father Ned explained that it was a Station Mass Ernie could not have been more co-operative.

I'll sign off now. That's all I have to say. I'm too busy to write more.

Your humble servant,
Martin MacMeer.

Editorial Dept.,
Irish Observer.

Dear Martin,

You can't be that busy. For pity's sake drop me a line. I'm only just getting to grips with public house life at this stage. I'm just getting to know the characters. When did Madge Dewley's husband die? Did she have a family? The Widow McGuire? What age is she? I know I'm asking a bit much but I'm dead curious as I am trying to formulate a pattern for a book.

Briege is alright, a little peaked sometimes but that's to be expected when you consider her condition. Write soon.

As ever,
Dan.

Journey's End,
Knockanee.

Dear Dan,

We are in the middle of an early August heatwave. Things are quiet till evening. Every rational holiday-maker is stretched below on the beach or bathing beyond at the Point. It is a lovely day with the faintest suggestion of breeze from the west and a blue sky without a speck of cloud. It's a day for all ages, to suit all tastes. Before I proceed further let me tell you that I am badly marked about the head and face after the August week-end. A number of youths came in here and tried to oust the other customers, in short tried to take over. I went outside the counter and asked them to leave. When I opened the door to usher them out one hit me from behind with an ashtray. Several of his accomplices joined in and I was beaten senseless. The same gang wrecked the Widow McGuire's and caused a serious disturbance at the Stella Maris. We all refused to serve them, all except Dixie Megley. If he had refused they would never again come to Knockanee. Later that night he had to run to the barracks for Civic Guards. I wonder what sort of homes these inhuman little wretches come out of or do they behave in those homes the way they do outside.

Today's parents are the main cause of teenage violence. They should have tamed these animals before unleashing them on an innocent public. What they do is turn their backs and wash their hands.

The Judas publican who serves under age youngsters with intoxicating drink must take his share of the blame too. These kids just cannot cope with strong drink. I've seen teenage girls endeavouring to practise the world's oldest trade after drinks in certain public houses.

Worse than this, of course, is the publican who serves the early morning prowler. Let me explain. As soon as it's light a hunger for drink consumes certain unfortunate gentlemen. They will scour the pubs of a town or village before their breakfasts looking for a pub that's open. As always there is one Judas. These unfortunates who need the drink are not evil people. They need help and they need it from publicans as much as they need it from everybody else. I have seen them with grey, wrinkled, unshaven faces prowling the streets and alleys. Most pubs will say no but we have that small, abominable handful who will do anything to make a sale. It is criminal to serve men like these who have no solid food in their stomachs. I once asked another publican why he did it.

'Because the man was sick and needed a cure,' he said.

'But what of his wife and family?' I entreated. 'What about his job?'

He did not answer. He could not. To answer your questions. Freddie Dewley, Madge's late husband, said his last goodbye to these climes in the winter of nineteen-sixty. He died from drink. It is as simple as that. There was no family. There had been a boy who was knocked down and killed by a car at the age of four. Neither Madge nor Freddie were heavy drinkers before that. In fact Madge never frequented pubs and Freddie's limit was a few pints of stout at week-ends. It was the loss of the little boy who was, by every account, a bright, intelligent, lovable little fellow that led them to drink.

I haven't seen Madge with a few days. She lets her house for the summer and lives in a little annex till the visitors have gone.

The Widow McGuire is a fine woman of about fifty who looks forty and she has an imposing bosom, lovely red hair without a grey rib. How she keeps it red is her business. She runs a good pub where a man can drink in peace and be sure of what he's getting. There's always some dicey drink going the rounds. Any port which shelters foreign trawlers also shelters a share of dubious brandy which is distributed cutely from time to time to certain publicans.

The Widow McGuire was married to the late Martin McGuire, a decent skin. He was drowned one pleasant July evening while collecting lobsters from his pots off the Point. Like most fishermen he could not swim a stroke. Some say he probably received a bite from a conger eel trapped in a lobster pot and that

he recoiled so violently he must have fallen backwards into the water. The Widow has two sons, Tom
the older is studying medicine at Cork University
and Wally the younger is still at secondary school.

Your friend and mine, Peadar Lyne, is boozing
away quietly and knocking off lonely middle-aged
female visitors by the new time. No wonder he never
married. We had a good season generally apart from
the trouble at the week-ends. Teenage drinking is
going to be a national problem in a few years. On
the sexual side Knockanee is no worse than any other
seaside resort. Stories may circulate but there is little
change in the relationships between your average boy
and girl. There will always be loose women but I
think these are the exceptions that prove the rule that
the vast majority of our girls are decent in the
extreme.

From time to time scandal breaks like a giant wave,
unexpected and refreshing. The latest worthwhile
stories concern Lily Lingley who is enraptured by a
young wavy-haired band vocalist of twenty-one and
Surgeon Casby who is never seen lately without a
young blonde who can't be out of her teens yet. These
are but the poppies in the wheatfield however, the
bad pennies that keep turning up, the nettles amongst
the potato stalks.

The trek from the beach is starting as the gentle
Atlantic breeze grows cooler and the first chill puffs
of the winds of evening alight on the near bare brown
bodies of bathers and beach addicts. Times have not
really changed as far as the relationship between men
and women is concerned. Men and women will always
lust after each other given the proper climate. However, all these things pass and life goes on regardless.

As ever,
Martin.

No new address yet,

Its me Peadar one from Cunnacanewer thick red legs
you must have seen her fair enough oul figure cook
at the Stella Maris Im after rising a flag there she
announced last night theres more marksmen in town
says I oh no says she Im not that kind that I'd be
a target like you'd see in a carnival for every pellet
gun around. Cant be sure would say she was round
the course before a few times and wound up in
winners enclosure I told her bolt a bottle of gin and
have a hot bath not that kind but as little says she
cant go home and tell father and mother and worse
still brothers working at Killclough Quarry look like
gorillas tear you apart Id swear just for the gas of
it one solution at present hit for Kilburn and go to
ground until storm blows over maybe she might lose
you know Cunnacanewer crowd as well as me so what
better for me to do. Tooraloo Ill see you before
Christmas tell stout woman widow Missus Goody
from Belfast staying at hotel will not be able meet her
tonight previous appointment.

Your oul segocia,
Peadar.

Will send address let me know lie of land.

Peadar.

Apt. 5-B.,
Sesame Arms Hotel,
Woodison Park,
New York.

Dear Martin,
Don't worry. This will be short and to the point.
I will be home very soon. You are not my 'Humble
Servant' as you said in your letter although I am
flattered that you so prostrate yourself.
One of the Embassy crowd here, a secretary aged

about forty with a bright diplomatic future, took me to dinner one night last week and again this week. I would not go out with him the third time although his intentions are honourable.

He has me persecuted for the last few days. Finally I had to tell him the sober truth, that there was somebody else. I want to be fair to you and true to you. I will not be seeing him again. For the present take care. I will be home on the 3rd of October which is only six weeks away. I'll come down the first weekend.

Now you have to admit that was not very long. Goodbye love,

xxxxxxxxxx
xxxxxxxxxx
Grace.

Journey's End,
Knockanee.

Dear Dan,

The big news is that Peadar Lyne is married. She is Fidelma Belton from Cunnacanewer. Everybody says he is lucky to have married such a fine girl. I was his bestman at a simple ceremony. The knot was tied by Father Ned Hauley. In sprinting parlance you might say that Peadar went off before the shot and was punished by being brought back to the starting line where he will now remain until he or Fidelma gives up the ghost and from the look of Fidelma she won't be giving up the ghost for a long time.

Peadar returned rather unexpectedly from England where he had been for a few days. He returned with two of Fidelma's brothers who invited him home to marry their sister.

So much for that. I am being driven into an almost indefensible position by Grace Lantry. She now presumes she has an understanding with me. I never met such a woman. What am I to do? I have stopped writing to her but I don't believe that will do any good either. She will be coming home in less than six weeks and it is her avowed intention to come down here the minute she returns. I cannot flee from here. I have to stand my ground. I have a business to run. I wish I could do a skip to Malu like any other cornered wretch. Love to Briege.

As ever,
Martin.

Editorial Dept.,
Irish Observer.

Dear Martin,
You have my sympathy. One statement in your letter amuses me. You say you never 'met such a woman'. There are thousands of Grace Lantrys ever hovering over likely prospects using every wile, every base dodge to turn what was an innocent friendship into a liaison of permanent misery. On at least three different occasions I was almost walked into it by the likes of Grace Lantry. I had to face tears, threats of suicide and God knows what. Each time, after a most harrowing period of constant soul-destroying assault, I was lucky to escape. Finally I met a woman I wanted to marry.

My advice is stand fast. Hold on to your territories and strengthen your redoubts and redans. Entrench yourself in the stressed concrete of the negative answer and be ever vigilant. A moment off guard could spell your downfall. Relax your vigilance for a second and the jig is up. Finally, never underestimate your enemy. If you do you will pay the price.

You mention teenage drinking in the context of national problems. Can nothing be done?

Love from all here,
Dan.

Journey's End,
Knockanee.

Dear Dan,
   You asked about teenage drinking. You always have
had the problem since the crushing of the first grape
but in those early times it was done within the com-
mune or family so that it rarely grew out of hand.
When I was a teenager there were scares and woeful
predictions. There was plenty teenage drinking. I
drank myself. I was lucky because drink agreed with
me and I knew when to stop. I cannot say the same
for many of my companions.
   What parents and teachers fail to grasp in these days
of affluence and drink-availability is that, in order to
succeed at any given pursuit, there must be training
beforehand. If the teenage drinker is to be a successful
drinker he must be coached. By successful drinker I
mean a boy or girl who is not violent, abusive, or irre-
sponsible in drink; a boy or girl who drinks in modera-
tion at certain prescribed times such as weddings, local
festivals and family celebrations. That is the primary
function of alcoholic drink, i.e. to complement happy
occasions and to add more cheer to parties and func-
tions. Drink has other uses but I will not go into these
now.
   To drive a motor car a young man must be taught
first how to drive, drilled in road regulations and made
to acquire considerable experience in car handling
before submitting to a rigid test. To otherwise inflict
him upon his fellows would be murderous.
   Should not the same code apply to intoxicating
drink? Alcohol is as potentially dangerous a weapon as
a motor car. Yet the tragedy is that youngsters often
embark on a night's drinking with no previous experience of carrying drink. The result of course is nearly
always disaster. Still it goes on despite the fact that
alcoholic beverages unwisely consumed can set boys

and girls on the high road to moral and physical collapse.

It is my experience as a publican that where you have a father drinking with his son there is rarely any danger of that boy's future in respect of alcoholism. This is supervised drinking, carefully, skilfully guided instruction in the art of social drinking. If the father takes the interest or the mother in the case of the daughter there is little danger of later over-indulgence when the boys and girls go out in the world. I can only speak from my own experience. Only the parents can point out the pitfalls, show by example that strong drink can be used to enjoy oneself and not to ultimately destroy self and others.

Another danger which I have noticed is the evil influence of thugs and bullies who advocate drunkenness as a virtue, i.e. judging a fellow by the amount of drink he can carry. This, of course, is an atrocious yardstick. I will stick to what I believe about parents guiding their offspring through the dangerous tides and shallows of alcoholism to the safe shore of general sobriety. Let the parent be the pilot and his family will be safe from the ravages of stupefaction, poverty and ill-health. In short they will instinctively know the way to a safe anchorage when caught amid the heavy seas of drunken sessions. Conversely it is similar to dropping a ball of paper into the depths of the ocean. For a while it will bob gaily and wilfully all over the surface but slowly the salt sea will penetrate to its core and there is nothing but a bloated mass which must disintegrate inevitably.

So to parents I would say this. To spare your young the agony of alcoholism, be by their sides when they most need you.

Love to Briege and the kids.

As ever,
Martin.

Kilteary Lodge Hotel,
Kilteary,
West Cork.

On the honeymoon weather you could say perfect
grub good but could do with more meat cut too thin
paddling to-day picked a few periwinkles ashamed to
ask hotel boil them its all before me now isnt it
couldnt be nicer to tell the truth the way she tries but
would rather pick my own apple than have it picked
for me still you'd have to like her shes for a fellow on
his side if you know what i mean and on the gay side
a weak bed id make no battle with her sent cards to
Madge Eva the widow and all the gang check up on
my property see you Monday bar a fall.

Your oul segocia,
Peadar and Fidelma.

Journey's End,
Knockanee.

Dear Dan,
I have a tragic tale to tell. On Sunday last Madge
Dewley appeared as usual with her bottles for the
cake and trifle ingredients. She looked wan and miserable as if she had endured a severe illness. When I
taxed her with this she cut loose and called me a
baldy ram. She pulls no punches. I advised her against
taking so much as she did not seem at all well. I
offered her brandy but she argued that she was entitled
to respect at her age. I was immediately sorry and I
filled her bottles. That night there was a fire in the
little annex where she lived across the summer and
autumn. She was badly burned and died before anyone could get to her. The only worthwhile possession
she had, apart from the decrepit furniture was a
locket and chain which she wore around her neck.
When I opened the locket there was a picture of her

husband and the little boy they lost in the accident.

I will say no more except that I pray the three are together again.

As ever,
Martin.

Editorial Dept.,
Irish Observer.

Dear Martin,

An idea has occurred to me apropos your position with the possessive Miss Lantry. Here is what I suggest. I will write her an anonymous letter in which I will reveal that I am a devout Catholic mother who has known you all your life. I would inform her that you are a known sheep and hen-rapist and petty thief with deep-seated homicidal tendencies. That shouldn't be long in putting a damper on her ardour.

Another approach would be to write and say that I am the mother of your half-grown, half-starved, badly-wronged child. If the position becomes desperate you will have to take desperate steps. Let me know what you think.

Now will you let me have an account of the burial of Madge Dewley? Who attended? What was the general reaction?

Briege was never better. She wants to know when you are coming to see us.

As ever,
Dan.

Journey's End,
Knockanee.

Dear Dan,

The funeral of Madge Dewley was one of the biggest in living memory. Cunnacanewer turned out in force as did the whole population of Knockanee.

It transpired that she had no sister married to a post-man in Cork. In fact she had no sister at all nor does there seem to be a trace of a living relative. The little annex in which she died was filled with old newspapers which caught fire while she was drunk. In fact she used these as bedclothes. It was a terribly threadbare place, reeking with poverty. The house itself was not too bad. There were beds and chairs and a table but beyond that little else of value. This is true of the houses of most heavy drinkers. The little ornaments of brass, glass, copper and china that are the outward symbols of moderate wealth elsewhere are nowhere to be seen. No treasures are hoarded in the long travail through life. There is little evidence of the trappings of independence. In most cases nothing at all remains. The moneys that would normally be used to buy bric-à-brac of one kind or another go to buy drink for one purpose or another. In the case of Madge the purpose was to shut out the memory of the husband and child she loved. She drank to forget. Others drink, believe it or not, in an effort to remember lost, loved ones or occasions of love and joy. There are those who drink out of pure selfishness. More unluckily for them, are possessed of enormous and insatiable appetites for intoxicating liquor. Some drink because of disillusion-ment whether it be marital or sexual or common everyday failure. In the side effects of this drinking is where the awful tragedy is most apparent in the wives who have to forego normal style for want of pocket money and who say nothing because of pride or shame, in the children who die the death every day from embarrassment of every conceivable kind, in the everlasting miserable, grinding poverty of every drunk-ard's dependant, in the hopeless, shameful, degrading, dehumanising day-to-day struggle to make ends meet and in the non-stop shouldering of the back-breaking burdens.

In the middle of all this is the publican. Not all

publicans see or know what is happening behind the scenes in the world of compulsive drinking. Some are insensitive. Others like myself who know and feel and sense the trouble do what we can but in cold analysis our positions are somewhat desperate. Yet publicans are there and are legally entitled to stay there. It is a tough job that might be bearable in spite of the long hours and the danger of assaults and the abuse if only we could be sure that we were not doing wrong from time to time. We cannot be blamed for alcoholism but there is much we can do, much we can prevent.

The only true salvation for the alocholic is that incomparable body of great souls known as the A.A. There are many who do not want to hear of it but therein lies the only salvation for otherwise incurable drinkers.

Madge is gone. She might say, if she were alive, that the drop of drink made life bearable for her. She might have turned to her God like other women and there found partial solace or at least enough to survive. She chose her own road. We buried her 'dacent' as they say. She deserved to be buried thus for she never lost her dignity.

This, in the last analysis, is the nub of the question, this basic matter of human dignity. Without it there can be no such thing as a worthwhile existence. There is nothing to equal the honour and the elevation of mind and character that is to be found in the dignity of man and woman. This massive virtue is corroded by excessive drinking. Gone is all the illustrious heritage of true humanity, the gravity, the nobility, the exaltation, the justifiable pride in one's own strength of character. The great stag that is human dignity is humbled and dragged down by the hounds of self-indulgence.

When dignity goes there is nothing left. Be sure that drunkenness and dignity cannot stay together in the same body. It's as simple as that.

About Grace Lantry. I doubt if she would be duped by a letter of the kind you mention, nor would she, in my opinion, be the least bit affected by the revelations you propose. I'll keep in touch concerning her.

Love to Briege and the kids,
As ever,
Martin.

Greenfields Hotel,
Highfield Parade,
Cork.

Dear Martin,
I have left Knockanee temporarily. My reason for so doing is that I want to think. You know Ernie Saschbuck who drinks at the Widow McGuire's? Of course you do. He wants to marry me. He is over seventy and I am only forty. Do you think we would have any chance together? I am not worried about his ability to perform the customary duties. I expect him to try his heart out and we all know the world loves a trier. The question I want you to answer if you can is this. I don't know how to put it. We've always been such good friends you and I. Well this is it.

I would not dream of marrying him if you disapproved. I would do anything you ask. I think you know that. That is why I am writing to you. If you would rather I should not marry him I will return home at once and tell him we will never share the same bed together. I will not, however, return to Knockanee until I hear from you.

You dear lifelong friend,
Eva St. George.

P.S. : Not a word to anyone. You know what they

would say. I can see the word abortion fluttering on their lips as they grimace at one another when news of my absence spreads.

Eva.

Journey's End,
Knockanee.

Dear Dan,
   Women. Women. Women. What predators they are. We have vilified innocent sharks and stalking tigers who seek only to have a decent meal but we have glorified women, the most incessant and possessive predators of all. We have put prices on the heads of foxes and squirrels but we allow women to rove about freely, seeking whatever prey they may presently fancy.

   Seriously Dan. I have a letter from Eva St. George which should be framed. At sixty-two years of age she professes to be forty and is worried lest people might imagine her to be pregnant. I wrote to her a while ago in answer to a letter which she sent me from Greenfields Hotel in Cork. Eva St. George pregnant! A regiment of the French Foreign Legion exiled for a year backed up by the crews of two aircraft carriers at sea for another year wouldn't put her by way of child.

   She asked me if she should marry Ernie Saschbuck who is eighty and growing mankier by the day. I answered by return and told her she should wed him at once. The sooner the better as far as I'm concerned. I feel I have struck another blow for my personal freedom. I'll write shortly. Love to Briege and the kids.

As ever,
Martin.

76

Old Point House,
Beach Road,
Knockanee.

Dear Martin,
 Jim and I will be married twenty-one years on
Saturday. We are having a few friends in for a bite
of supper and a drink or two. We would love to have
you along in view of our old friendship. Let me know
within the next few days. Jim bids me to tell you
that he will be most disappointed if you don't show
up.

Sincerely,
Lily Lingley.

Journey's End,
Knockanee.

Dear Dan,
 Peadar is well settled now in Knockanee and seems
mightily pleased with himself. As I write there is a
storm rising and the sea is a mass of swirly grey foam.
Far out I can discern a tanker as she battles her way
towards Limerick. Seagulls drift inland before the
gale and the torn clouds tumble recklessly overhead.
It's nice to be seated snugly indoors on a day like this.
In comes a tiny man by the name of Bluney, Jerry
Bluney. Already I have several other customers and
all look up eagerly to see how I will react to Bluney
who, incidentally, is nicknamed the Holy Terror. He
is the most inoffensive and mildest little man imagin-
able, the most likeable and lovable little person who
ever drew breath, a deeply religious little gentleman
who haunts the chapel, a smiling, harmless soul until
he gets two pints of porter inside him.
 Then he is a little demon, a vicious, treacherous
blackguard who will shout his way home challenging
all-comers and waking people from their well-earned
repose. It's a mystery to me that he hasn't been killed

years ago. I take perverse pleasure in refusing him for a pint. I adopt the same angelic smile that he wears himself and in a sugary voice I tell him that I will not serve him. With a polite nod he withdraws. Later tonight he will stand outside my door on his way home with a few pints of porter inside him.

'Come out, you cowardly baldy bastard,' he will shout at the top of his voice. 'Come out, till I tear your heart out. Come out, you spoiled priest, you cut-jack till I throttle you.'

That's just a sample. A cut-jack, by the way, is a stallion ass or in electrical terms an ass whose light bulb has been taken from its socket or, if you like, a donkey with a diminished undercarriage.

In Knockanee also there is another tiny gentleman whose name is Roderick or Roddy O'Dill. Roderick is known locally as the White Hope. Ever since Jack Johnson defeated Tommy Burns and became the first black man to win the heavyweight championship of the world white sports fans have clamoured for a White Hope, that is to say a white heavyweight who would wrest the title from the negroes. It is my contention that no white man would ever have held the title if black boxers had been give equal opportunity but I think all sportsmen know this.

Later when Louis dominated the scene there was further clamour. About this time Roddy O'Dill was brought into court by his wife to defend a charge of assault and battery. Arriving home drunk one night he demanded that the frying pan be taken out and that sausages, puddings, kidney, etc., be fried for him. When his wife pointed out that he had neglected to provide her with the wherewithal to purchase any sort of provision he assumed a fighting stance and struck her a blow on the mouth. She fell to the ground.

In court his defence was that he mistook her for Joe Louis because he had more than his share of drink taken.

'Another white hope,' said the justice and the name stuck. Wherever he went thereafter he was called the White Hope, derisively, of course, because no man loves a wife beater. Many an honest man often drew a belt at his beloved but that was that. They never made a habit of it. So did many an honest woman flatten her partner with a blow from a suitable kitchen utensil but that was the end of it and there was a making-up of great proportions.

For years the White Hope staggered home on week-end nights boasting to all and sundry as follows: 'I am the White Hope. I have beaten my wife two hundred and fifty-seven times and tonight I will beat her for the two hundred and fifty-eighth.'

So saying the drunken little wretch would stagger home and if she was there before him he would insult her or assault her according to his mood. In his fighting career he had over three hundred victories and only one defeat. His defeat came about this way. His family, apart from his unfortunate wife, consisted of one son and two daughters.

One night he came home drunk and aggressive. He demanded meat but there was none to be had. He first started to berate her and then he started to pummel her. He forgot one thing. During all the years of beatings his son had been slowly growing into a man. When he heard his mother's cries he became frightened as always but then slowly and inevitably a great fury took hold of him. He came downstairs and told his mother to go upstairs. She did as she was bade. The son then inflicted the following injuries upon his father: two black eyes a broken nose, a fractured jaw and three fractured ribs. He went upstairs and kissed his mother and sisters before leaving home. He was never seen again in Knockanee. After that the White Hope never laid a glove on his wife nor did he ever take an intoxicating drink.

If the district justice had been less facetious and more just on that far-off court-day and handed him a month in jail the son might never have been called upon to do what he had to do.

I have an invitation to a twenty-first wedding anniversary at Lingleys'. I'll let you know all about it in due course. Love to Briege and the kids.

As ever,
Martin.

Wellington Heights,
Dublin.

My dear Martin,

I have just arrived back in Dublin. I will be down on the week-end after next. I look forward more than I can say to seeing you. All I ask, seriously, is that you don't throw me out. I have some most interesting local news which I shall not put down on paper. You don't have to worry about my motives. I have no intention of railroading you. I just want to spend a quiet week-end with my favourite people. I have a lovely wedding present for Peadar and his bride. I have another for Ernie and Eva. Eva did well for a girl of sixty. I'll say no more for now, dear Martin.

xxxxxxxxxxxxxx
xxxxxxxxxxxxxx
xxxxxxxxxxxxxx
xxxxxxxxxxxxxx
Your dear friend,
Grace.

Journey's End,
Knockanee.

Dear Dan,

You-know-who is back but, apart from a hundred or so kiss-crosses, seems to have lost the initiative. Amen say I. She hasn't alighted here yet but is due shortly.

There was intense activity by the Civic Guards here on Sunday night. Following a spate of poison pen letters, probably written by an envious publican, all the pubs were raided. The letters, of course, could have been written by a housewife who is getting no money to run the house but my guess is that it was a publican whose business has fallen off. We have such a publican here. Journey's End was mentioned in one of the letters. I was accused of serving drink to under-age customers at all hours of the morning.

The Widow McGuire was the first to be raided. The time was ten-thirty which is a half hour after the legal closing time. When Mick Henderson was granted access by the Widow's son he was astonished at what he saw. Kneeling all over the bar were hatless men of all ages. The Widow was reciting the Rosary and the assembly was diligently answering.

'Guards on public house duty,' Mick announced. Then he addressed himself to the Widow.

'How can you account,' said he, 'for the presence of these men on your premises?' No answer from the Widow. Together with the Guard who accompanied him Mick knelt down and answered the Rosary like all the rest. When it was finished Mick repeated his question : 'How can you account for these men on your premises?'

'We were saying the Rosary,' said the Widow.

'In honour of what?' asked Mick.

'For the Pope's intentions,' said the Widow. Since there was no sign of intoxicating drink to be seen and since Mick didn't really want to catch the Widow he cautioned her and warned her that there were to be no more after-hours Rosaries. He then cleared the house. I was next on his list. There were Peadar, Ernie Saschbuck, my Uncle Matt and three of his Cunnacanewer cronies. First came the knock at the door. Then came the announcement 'Guards on public house duty.' The three Cunnacanewer men, as if they had been rehearsing for years, silently swept all drinks from the table and disappeared upstairs. Immediately I opened the door. Mick entered followed by Guard Batty Cronin.

'How can you account,' asked Mick, 'for the presence of these men on your premises?'

'They are all authorised persons,' I answered. 'Peader works here part-time as you know and this man is my uncle and resident here.'

I must confess that I was stuck as far as Ernie Saschbuck was concerned. Mick, however, came to my aid.

'And this man,' said he, 'is an American Citizen.'

Batty and he then bade us goodnight and went off about their business. The Stella Maris was packed and there was a roaring sing-song which could be heard on the street. From everyone's point of view this was considered fair game so names were taken and the licensee charged. The last pub to be raided that night was Micky Holohan's at the other end of Tipplers' Terrace. He had heard on the grapevine that Guards were raiding but like many another foolish publican he never dreamed that he would be visited himself. When the knock came Micky moved all his customers into his aged mother's bedroom and lighted two candles on a table next to the bed. Next he placed a crucifix in the old woman's hands and tucked a missal under her chin.

'Play dead,' Micky told her. The old woman was as frail as a starving bird. She looked the part. The customers stood round respectfully with their drinks in their hands. A look of mourning appeared on each face. Micky went downstairs where he admitted the sergeant and guard.

'Anyone on the premises?' asked Mick Henderson.

'Just a few friends,' said Micky 'my poor mother passed on a short while back and there's no one in the wake-room bar mourners.'

'You have my deepest sympathy,' said Mick, 'you will take no exception I'm sure if Guard Cronin says a prayer over her. I'm a bad warrant to climb stairs lately.'

'He'll be most welcome,' said Micky gratefully. Head bent in sorrow he led the way upstairs and found a place, far from the bed, where the Guard could kneel in comfort. In the weak candlelight the old lady looked like a corpse. Batty Cronin was convinced. Clutching his cap in his hand he left the room. In the street afterwards as he and the sergeant wended their majestic way towards the Barracks the older man spoke confidentially. 'You know something, Batty,' said Mick Henderson, 'it wouldn't surprise me one bit if that old lady were to rise from the dead shortly.'

Micky Holohan's mother, as prophesied by the sergeant, did rise from the dead and Micky to give him his due was down to the barracks first thing in the morning to reveal the joyful news.

'It must have been a coma she was in then,' said Mick Henderson.

'The very thing,' said Mickey Holohan, who wouldn't know a coma from a running nose. ' 'Twas a coma for sure.'

'Anything is better than a full-stop, Micky,' chimed in Batty Cronin who had been listening in the day-room.

I have a visitor. There is something about him. He did not walk in. He sidled in silently. He looks the very epitome of humility, a shabby excuse for what he should be or might have been or what he once was. You gather at once that he is kind and gentle. You know immediately that he would never make a fuss. His pale cheeks are indrawn. Somewhere along the line, in his quest for liquor, he lost his false teeth and, I would suspect, his spectacles for there is a red trace across the upper of his nose. He could do with a shave and a new raincoat. I daresay he could do with a whole new body. He is most respectful, the relict of old decencies, as they say in Cunnacanewer.

'A small Irish and a bottle of stout.' He places the money meticulously on the counter. I serve him and he swallows. He literally melts with relief before my eyes. Now I'm sure that he is an alcoholic. I call Peadar to ring a number in Listowel. Help will be along shortly.

I had better sign off and take charge of this man. Love to Briege and the kids.

As ever,
Martin.

Compassionate Convent,
Knockanee.

Dear Martin,

I so enjoyed the Lingley party the other night. It was so old-fashioned it took me back to parties I attended as a child in the great house of an Ascendancy neighbour. Everything was done in style and dignity and songs like The Last Rose of Summer and Greensleeves were accorded pride of place. I liked your rendition of the Foster songs particularly The Old Kentucky Home. What an accomplished pianist Surgeon Casby is. Martin, it's a long time since we had a chat. Come and see me on Saturday morning.

I am out of touch with events for the past few weeks, ever since the retreat. The town could be burned down and I wouldn't know about it.

Please bring a bottle of brandy, a dozen stout, a bottle of your best sherry and a dozen of assorted minerals. Also I would like if you tendered your full account as from Christmas last. We must owe you a small fortune. Take care of yourself.

Yours in J.C.,
Mother Martha.

P.S. : Deliver the goods and the bill at the rear entrance. Then come to the front. The hall door will be open. Walk straight through to the sitting-room.

M.M.

Journey's End,
Knockanee.

Dear Dan,

Christmas is coming. Therefore, you will find a lull in the letter-writing as business usually improves across the season. Grace Lantry has come and gone. She is due back again for Christmas. She stays with Peadar and the wife as a paying guest. This time she did not push herself. She was content to remain in the background. Would you say that she is a reformed, new Grace Lantry or the old Grace with a new bag of tricks? I think that she has calmed down a lot as a result of her American visit. I am prepared to accept her on that basis. I shall, of course, not shed a whit of my usual vigilance.

The party at Jim and Lily Lingleys was an outstanding success. It was attended by what the Lingleys believed to be the more refined elements in the village. If you don't mind I sang a selection of Foster's songs from De Camptown Races through Old Virginia to The Old Kentucky Home where I closed the door. Needless to mention I was nicely tanked up. I'll say one thing for Lily, she has a liberal hand with a bottle. Among the guests were Mother Martha, Father Hauley, Father Dee the curate, Doctor Sugan, Ernie and Eva Saschbuck, Surgeon and Mrs Casby who drove from Cork for the occasion, Mick Henderson and his wife, the Widow McGuire, Peadar Lyne and his wife as a concession to me and quite a few others whose names do not come to mind immediately. There was a buffet-style supper with every conceivable delicacy. I recall lobster, crab and escallop. There was salmon and sea trout. I saw turkey, tongue, beef, ham, mutton and a variety of salads. Some stuffed themselves. I am certain that they must have suffered afterwards. I swear I never saw such glaring examples of gluttony, mostly by the better off, believe it or not. Buffets always terrify me for the rampant near-cannibalism that goes on, the unmitigated greed and the ungoverned gorging. I had a satisfying meal and plenty of drink afterwards but some who should know better had to be carted home. If you wanted to get rid of these elements permanently the thing is to offer them a succession of invitations to buffets. As long as the victuals and liquor are free they will always overdo it. It would be a mere matter of time before they eventually succumbed to gluttony.

We were all photographed together for the local paper and the photographer went around afterwards asking for our names. I'm certain we will be painstakingly dissected by the locals as soon as the paper comes out on Friday. That is the price of fame even if it is fame for a day only. It must be great to be a half-wit or a recluse or to be habitually in the background or to be a dodger. No responsibility and one is answerable to nobody. One's advice is never sought. One is never asked to stand at a church gate or sit upon a platform. Yet one can be part of it all and enjoy the occasional discomfiture or destruction of those who take part or take sides. I suppose the truth is that most people are like this. The others are merely the entertainers. I will sign off now and write as soon as I have anything of importance. Love to Briege and the kids.

As ever,
Martin.

Wellington Heights,
Dublin.

Dear Martin,
    I expect to be down next week-end. I want you to

promise me something. Under no circumstances enter any bonds or agreements, engagements or bargains until I see you. If you do your life will be a shambles before you know it. I am not at liberty to convey the explosive news which I have recently heard. Let me give you a final warning. Make no promises of any kind to anybody until we meet face to face. You can do as you please then.

Your dear and faithful friend,
Grace.

Journey's End,
Knockanee.

Dear Dan,

Antoinette Lingley is home. She is a chastened, cowed rather sad Antoinette. Yet in a way she is more beautiful. I think she may have been blamed in the wrong. I am not saying that she is an angel. What I would suggest is that she was easily led, being an innocent and credulous girl with no experience of the world. The other day I went to visit Mother Martha at the convent and we had a long chat about the village and about the goings-on. She filled me in on any number of matters of which I was ignorant. She produced a bottle of brandy and poured a few stiff doses for me. She never touches a drop herself. She told me her father had been a confirmed drunkard. While we were chatting who should arrive but Lily Lingley who informed us that Antoinette was home and would, most likely, be staying home and helping her father in the office.

Mother Martha insisted we both stay for lunch. She pressed a convenient wall button and in a matter of seconds a shining-faced nun appeared. Martha informed her that the visitors' dining-room was to be made ready. After another brandy we repaired to the dining-room where we were served with an excellent leek soup. There followed a main course of truly succulent roast beef, pot-roast potatoes and a variety of fresh vegetables. This was followed by a rich trifle, flavoured to a nicety with good quality sherry. Then came the coffee and then the chat.

When Antoinette left Knockanee in disgrace she went to a relation who employed her as a receptionist. You know all this. I recall telling you in an earlier letter. What you do not know is the following. Before her disgrace Antoinette was studying for all she was worth. The Leaving Certificate examination was her target. Weakened by non-stop studies and further bemused by parents who took it for granted that she was inviolate and therefore invulnerable, Antoinette was easy meat for the housemaid Kitty Bang-Bang.

Let me dwell for a while on the Bang-Bangs. They are indigenous to a place called Toorytooreen, a townland at the other side of Cunnacanewer hill. Their real names are Mulleys. Kitty Bang-Bang would be a daughter to Nellie Bang-Bang and Nellie Bang-Bang a daughter to Molly Bang-Bang who was first invested with the title. How old Molly whose real name was Shayton deserved to be so called nobody knows. One may safely deduce that it is not a nickname you would expect to see conferred on a member of the Children of Mary. No more will I say in this respect. Anyway Toorytooreen is noted for pishogues, black magic etcetera.

Before Kitty Bang-Bang came to work for the Lingley's Antoinette was a wide-eyed innocent. Before Kitty left Antoinette was a hardened woman of the world. Lily Lingley assured us that her daughter was first hypnotised and then doped by Kitty Bang-Bang. It seems logical anyway you look at it. How else can you account for the incredible transformation of innocence to evil. As a seasoned reporter you will have to agree that Antoinette's downfall was not entirely due

88

to herself. There had to be an outside force. These things do not just happen out of the blue.

Anyway to proceed with the story it transpired that Jim and Lily Lingley went one week-end to Killarney to a builders' conference. They spent three days away from home all told and upon their return Lily noticed that Antoinette looked a little drawn and appeared to be listless. She was not in the least worried at this stage as these periods of listlessness are common to all girls. She thought it was perfectly natural for Antoinette to look pale and wan at regular intervals. Across the spring Jim and Lily spent a number of week-ends in Dublin and Cork. They spent a week in London. Lily assured us that they would never have gone on these trips if they thought anything was amiss at home. It was during these absences that the orgies took place. Did I tell you that a number of obscene photographs were found in Antoinette's room afterwards. I have not seen these nor do I want to but Lily told us that if one was to judge from the expression of abandon and wantonness on Antoinette's face there could be no remaining doubt but that she was under the influence of some very potent drug whether shop-bought or home-brewed. My uncle Matt will tell you that there was a love potion, commonly called Coaxiorum, in wide use in Toorytooreen up to the late nineteen forties before the great guns of Europe blew a million myths and fables into total obscurity.

However, to press on I do not suggest for a minute that Coaxiorum was used. The point I would like to bring out is that some form of potion, drug or charm was used on Antoinette. Mother Martha, after hearing Lily's account of the business, declared that she was convinced that Antoinette was the victim of a fiendish intrigue between Kitty Bang-Bang and certain unscrupulous perverts who were prepared to stop at nothing to have their way with Antoinette. Martha then gave us a resume of Antoinette's career from the day she entered the convent to the afternoon of the balloon. The girl had been a model of perfection up to that fateful day.

I myself have no doubt about her innocence. I was too hasty to condemn her. The only excuse I can offer is that everybody else was doing it at the time and I was working on the obnoxious premise that if everybody says so it has to be.

Winter is here in real earnest, my friend. The seas have been murderous these past few days with foaming, mountainous breakers thundering ruthlessly on rock and beach. Love to Briege and the kids.

As ever,
Martin.

Sleepy Valley,
Knockanee.

Dear Grace,
Hop on your bike fast the jig is up they have your man rightly banjoed the reverend mother and Lily Lie Low and the balloon merchant with the face like Marie Goretti such a gang reverend mother innocent enough dont know her oats thats all say now the young wan doped by Kitty Bang-Bang all lies Bang-Bangs every bloody one of em decent oul skins would lie down alright but whats that this day and age and wholl gainsay not you or me for sure nor devil a man with red blood and sound tackling. Lingley outfit need no dope nor nothing else mother and daughter game to the tail bred for the caper nothin come out of a box faster Martin goes around moonin and broodin like he'd be suffocatin they have the sign put on him for sure better he be borned a rabbit he now surrounded on all sides no escape better you buzz down fast dont wait for starters orders or flag to go up or the man in black will have the knot tied oh yes seen the mother and Mrs Casby headin for Journey's End last night

fierce hurry throwin' the hot sups in all directions ho-
ho say I dont delay talk about sellin a jennet pretendin
tis a pony nothing the equal of Lily Lie Low you
might lift the leg but you wont pull it ho-ho say I
catch asleep a weasel very down to earth these days
all put on for Martin all moryah stand easy I was a
private myself if you twig all the blame now on Kitty
Bang-Bang poor cratur her grandmother got the nickname first poor Molly God be good to her fowlers up
that way scourin Toorytooreen for pheasants one
fowler chats up Molly nice slip of a girl then time pass
poor Molly showin the signs Molly no English in those
days all Irish in Cunnacanewer and Toorytooreen
father and mother quiz her hard who covered her
first bang bang said Molly meanin twas the fowler thats
the true story harmless poor people part the goods for a
bag of toffees no more bother no sense as I say God
help us all rich and poor no one the match for the
Lingley daughter the hardest case I ever came across
and I met a few in my time hard as the black rocks
smooth as Lochlune tricky like the sea herself you
have the law you might have a chance youll want all
you have Eva placed in good position daubin away up
the road a bit can see all comins and goins reports all
that goes on we cant hold out much longer all rockets
gone battery low last sos going down for third time
dont notify Martin poor man bewitched another
martyr for old Ireland another victim for the long
hairs.

> Your friend,
> Peadar Lyne.

Journey's End,
Knockanee.

Dear Dan,
    All hell has broken loose. The storm has come when

I least expected it and I am tossed like a cork right smack in the middle of the maelstrom harried by raving maenads not knowing where to turn. I am writing this in the loneliness of my bedroom. The door is locked for safety's sake. I don't want to be caught again in the terrible crossfire of female accusations.

Grace Lantry arrived last night. She came in the middle of the engagement party. Did I tell you I was engaged to the fair Antoinette for a few hours? Lantry soon put an end to that. There we were, all good friends, a jolly good company as the song says, when she arrives without a word of warning. Present were Antoinette and her mother and father together with their friends the Casbys and all the others who were at the anniversary party at Lingleys. I was seated outside the counter in the thick of the rejoicing. Eva and Peadar were behind the counter and we were all having a wonderful time. Grace said or did nothing for a while. She accepted the green Chartreuse which Peadar handed her and she seemed to relax. She sat near Surgeon Casby who promptly took his hand from Lily Lingley's knee and transferred it to Grace's. She lifted the hand and inflicted a sharp bite on it. Everybody else thought she had kissed it but I knew from Casby's face that he had been bitten. This should have forewarned me the way a ringed moon warns a sailor but I was sated with liquor and looking lustfully at the shapely young thing who was to be my bride. Time passed. A number of songs were sung. I myself contributed. A cold plate was handed to everyone. Lily, Mrs Casby and Mrs Lyne had prepared these earlier. There were numerous toasts. It was at the end of her toast that Grace made her onslaught. She literally took the Lingleys apart. She did it carefully and systematically. Her training had prepared her well.

Here is the cold truth backed by hard facts. Antoinette did not go to a relative in Dublin to act as his receptionist. She stole three hundred pounds from her father and went to London instead where she had an abortion. After a week's rest she went after a job. She had little difficulty in finding one as a photographer's model. The photographer had less difficulty in convincing Antoinette that her finer points deserved a wider audience. Grace produced some of the erotica in which Antoinette had been involved with some well-developed young gentlemen.

This was bad enough until Grace revealed that the younger Lingley, in a matter of months, became the most sought-after and expensive call-girl in London.

Why then you may well ask, my dear Dan, did she chose to abandon a calling for which she was ideally suited and which she thoroughly enjoyed. The answer is two-fold. Firstly she broke the rules. She spoke about her clients. Apparently this is something you can never do in this particular profession.

Secondly she acquired an unfortunate ailment common to the trade. Of this I will say no more. You are a man of the world. You will draw the correct conclusion. The aim was to foist her over on me. You would think that having been once bitten I would be twice shy. Alas no. I am a mere mortal, a thing of flesh and bone and temperament. I was snared a second time. But for Grace I would have been snared for eternity. If I had been married when she arrived she would not have told me. There but for the grace of God, my dear Dan, I would have gone. I will arise in a short while now and go to the Widow McGuire's where I will consume one large brandy. I will then walk towards the shore until I arrive at the abode of Jer Taxi. His correct name, of course, is not Jer Taxi but that is how he is called. I shall commission Jer Taxi to drive me to the town of Listowel. From there I propose to embark upon a long shaughrawn. It will be some time before you hear from me. I have the feeling anyhow that I am writing the closing chapter. It is a critical time for me. I feel that

93

Fate is closing in on me. I'll say no more for the nonce.

Love to Briege and the kids.

As ever,
Martin.

So it was that Martin MacMeer embarked upon his last and most memorable shaughrawn or, as he liked to call it himself, his purification pilgrimage. He was absent from Journey's End for a period of seventeen days which brought us up to a fortnight from Christmas. This final shaughrawn was something of a local record. In the town he bade farewell to Jer Taxi and proceeded to the lounge of an hotel where he was warmly received by his old friend Anna Stacey. At nine o'clock he left the hotel. We must rely on hearsay if we are to trace his movements after this. He was seen in a variety of places during the following seventeen days. If it was not he who was seen it was surely someone who bore a remarkable resemblance to him. In a letter from Glasgow he was the chief news. This letter was written to a Mrs Josie Maldowney of Tippler's Terrace by her sister Hannah who is married in Glasgow. She maintained that she saw him staggering past the Citizen's Theatre as she and her husband were leaving after a show. She called after him but he lurched off into the darkness taking enormous strides. He was positively identified by several Cunnacanewer and Knockanee exiles who saw him in places like Soho, Streatham, Cricklewood and The Strand. His eyes were glazed and he did not stop when called upon to do so. One witness wrote to say that there was a whiff of stale drink off him that would knock you down.

He was seen in Kilkee by moonlight and in the town of Nenagh in Tipperary a spirits salesman identified him leaving a hotel.

When he returned home to Journey's End, a worn and exhausted man, Grace Lantry was waiting for him. Aided by delicate broths and slight but highly palatable snacks she won him back to health. They married on the fifth day of January as soon as the Christmas season had all but expired. They now live happily in Knockanee and if we are to believe Peadar Lyne there will be napkins soon on the rusted clothes line which extends across the back yard of Journey's End.

More Interesting Titles

DURANGO

John B. Keane

Danny Binge peered into the distance and slowly spelled out the letters inscribed on a great sign in glaring red capitals:

'DURANGO,' he read

'That is our destination,' the Rector informed his friend. 'I'm well known here. These people are my friends and before the night is over they shall be your friends too.'

The friends in question are the Carabim girls: Dell, aged seventy-one and her younger sister, seventy-year-old Lily. Generous, impulsive and warm-hearted, they wine, dine and entertain able-bodied country boys free of charge – they will have nothing to do with the young men of the town or indeed any town ...

Durango is an adventure story about life in rural Ireland during the Second World War. It is a story set in an Ireland that is fast dying but John B. Keane, with his wonderful skill and humour, brings it to life, rekindling in the reader memories of a time never to be quite forgotten ...

LOVE BITES and other stories

John B. Keane

John B. introduces us to 'Corner Boys', 'Window Peepers', 'Human Gooseberries', 'Fortune-Tellers', 'Funeral Lovers', 'Female Corpses', 'The Girls who came with the Band' and many more fascinating characters.